CUMBRIA LIBRARIES
CUMBRIA LIBRARIES
KT-434-867

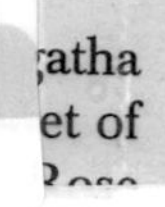

M. C. B… …gatha
Raisin a… …et of
Edwardian… …Rose

County Council
Libraries, books and more . . .

GRANGE | 11 FEB 2014 | 29 MAY 2014

'[Beaton] is adept at character portrayal and development . . . *Plain Jane* is sure to delight Regency enthusiasts of all ages.'

Best Sellers

'Once again the infamous town house on Clarges Street is occupied for a season . . . [Beaton] sets a lively tempo.'

Publishers Weekly

'A witty, charming, touching bit of Regency froth. Highly recommended.'

Library Journal

'Entertaining light romance for fans of the series.'

Booklist

'A romp of a story . . . For warm-hearted, hilarious reading, this one is a gem.'

Baton Rouge Sunday Advocate

Titles by M. C. Beaton

A House for the Season

The Miser of Mayfair • *Plain Jane* • *The Wicked Godmother*
Rake's Progress • *The Adventuress* • *Rainbird's Revenge*

The Six Sisters

Minerva • *The Taming of Annabelle* • *Deirdre and Desire*
Daphne • *Diana the Huntress* • *Frederica in Fashion*

The Edwardian Murder Mystery series

Snobbery with Violence • *Hasty Death* • *Sick of Shadows*
Our Lady of Pain

The Travelling Matchmaker series

Emily Goes to Exeter • *Belinda Goes to Bath* • *Penelope Goes to Portsmouth*
Beatrice Goes to Brighton • *Deborah Goes to Dover* • *Yvonne Goes to York*

The Agatha Raisin series

Agatha Raisin and the Quiche of Death • *Agatha Raisin and the Vicious Vet*
Agatha Raisin and the Potted Gardener • *Agatha Raisin and the Walkers of Dembley*
Agatha Raisin and the Murderous Marriage • *Agatha Raisin and the Terrible Tourist*
Agatha Raisin and the Wellspring of Death • *Agatha Raisin and the Wizard of Evesham*
Agatha Raisin and the Witch of Wyckhadden
Agatha Raisin and the Fairies of Fryfam • *Agatha Raisin and the Love from Hell*
Agatha Raisin and the Day the Floods Came
Agatha Raisin and the Curious Curate • *Agatha Raisin and the Haunted House*
Agatha Raisin and the Deadly Dance • *Agatha Raisin and the Perfect Paragon*
Agatha Raisin and Love, Lies and Liquor
Agatha Raisin and Kissing Christmas Goodbye
Agatha Raisin and a Spoonful of Poison • *Agatha Raisin: There Goes the Bride*
Agatha Raisin and the Busy Body • *Agatha Raisin: As the Pig Turns*

The Hamish Macbeth series

Death of a Gossip • *Death of a Cad* • *Death of an Outsider*
Death of a Perfect Wife • *Death of a Hussy* • *Death of a Snob*
Death of a Prankster • *Death of a Glutton* • *Death of a Travelling Man*
Death of a Charming Man • *Death of a Nag* • *Death of a Macho Man*
Death of a Dentist • *Death of a Scriptwriter* • *Death of an Addict*
A Highland Christmas • *Death of a Dustman* • *Death of a Celebrity*
Death of a Village • *Death of a Poison Pen* • *Death of a Bore*
Death of a Dreamer • *Death of a Maid* • *Death of a Gentle Lady*
Death of a Witch • *Death of a Valentine* • *Death of a Sweep*
Death of a Kingfisher

The Skeleton in the Closet

Also available
The Agatha Raisin Companion

Plain Jane

Being the Second Volume of
A House for the Season

M.C. Beaton

Canvas

Constable & Robinson Ltd
55–56 Russell Square
London WC1B 4HP
www.constablerobinson.com

First published in the US by St Martin's Press, 1986

This paperback edition published in the UK by Canvas,
an imprint of Constable & Robinson Ltd, 2013

Copyright © M. C. Beaton, 1986

The right of M. C. Beaton to be identified as the author of this work has been asserted by her in accordance with the Copyright, Designs and Patents Act 1988

All rights reserved. This book is sold subject to the condition that it shall not, by way of trade or otherwise, be lent, resold, hired out or otherwise circulated in any form of binding or cover other than that in which it is published and without a similar condition including this condition being imposed on the subsequent purchaser.

This is a work of fiction. Names, characters, places and incidents are either the product of the author's imagination or are used fictitiously, and any resemblance to actual persons, living or dead, or to actual events or locales is entirely coincidental.

A copy of the British Library Cataloguing in
Publication Data is available from the British Library

ISBN: 978-1-78033-306-9 (paperback)

Typeset by TW Typesetting, Plymouth, Devon

Printed and bound in the UK

1 3 5 7 9 10 8 6 4 2

For Raja

He was a type of strange breed of men which has vanished from England – the full-blooded virile buck, exquisite in his dress, narrow in his thoughts, coarse in his amusements, and eccentric in his habits. They walk across the bright stage of English history with their finicky step, their preposterous cravats, their high collars, their dangling seals, and they vanish into the dark wings from which there is no return. The world has outgrown them, and there is no place now for their strange fashions, their practical jokes, and carefully cultivated eccentricities. And yet behind this outer veiling of folly with which they so carefully draped themselves, they were often men of strong character and robust personality.

SIR ARTHUR CONAN DOYLE, *RODNEY STONE*

ONE

Society is now one polish'd horde,
Form'd of two mighty tribes, the bores and the bored.

LORD BYRON, *DON JUAN*

At the beginning of 1808, fog turned London into a nightmare city. It was not that a London fog was a rarity. What was so odd, so dismal, and so depressing was that it should last so long.

A choking yellow-grey blanket lay over the metropolis, turning day into night. Never had the link boys been so much in demand as they guided their charges through the stifling fog, lighting their way, their blazing torches reduced to mere red eyes of light through the encircling gloom.

Even the elegant streets of the West End had lost their light and airy character as carriages swam like great primeval beasts through the grey swamp, and figures darted to and fro like wraiths.

Passersby shied nervously away from the two great iron dogs chained on the steps outside

Number 67 Clarges Street, the sluggishly shifting fog making the animals look real.

Inside Number 67, the servants felt the fog had crept into their very souls, so grey and miserable did their lives seem. It was a new year and already they were on the threshold of another London Season. But the bad luck that had haunted the town house in Clarges Street continued to haunt it, and it looked as if they would lack a tenant, which meant no tips to augment their miserable wages.

The house was owned by the tenth Duke of Pelham, a young man who owned so much property, including a large mansion in Grosvenor Square, that he was barely aware of the house's existence. The management of the house, the letting of it, and the payment of the staff were left to his agent, Jonas Palmer, cheat, bully and liar.

Napoleon's armies held all Europe in an iron grip and threatened the security of Britain. Times were hard. Servants could not hope to find new employment without references. Palmer had said he would never give any of the servants at Number 67 references and, furthermore, he would give any planning to leave a bad character. This allowed him to continue to pay the staff very low wages while charging his master proper wages and putting the difference in his own pocket.

A good tenant was the servants' only hope. A generous tenant might raise their wages for the length of the rental and might even provide them with the necessary references. But their hopes of ever seeing another tenant were very slim.

Number 67 was damned as unlucky.

The ninth duke had hanged himself there. The year after that, the first family to rent the house for a Season had lost all their money through their son's gambling and the second tenants, the life of their beautiful daughter, Clara.

The third tenant, a Scottish gentleman, Mr Roderick Sinclair and his ward, Fiona, whom he had presented as his daughter, had been generous to the staff and good luck seemed to have come to the house at last. But Fiona Sinclair had married the Earl of Harrington and had gone abroad with him on their honeymoon. They had disappeared without trace and were feared dead.

Once more the house was advertised in the daily newspapers.

A HOUSE FOR THE SEASON
Gentleman's residence, 67
Clarges Street, Mayfair.
Furnished town house. Trained
servants. Rent: £80 sterling.
Apply, Mr Palmer, 25 Holborn.

It was possible to rent a house in a middling part of the town for £80 for a whole year. But in Mayfair, where one could expect to pay at least £1,000 a year rent for unfurnished and unstaffed accommodation, the sum of £80 for the few months of the

Season was very modest. Most hopeful mamas arrived in London some time before the Season began, to lay the ground for their daughters' coming-out. Therefore anyone in the *ton* knew that a house rented for the Season included two months before and at least one after. The Season began at the end of April and lasted until the end of June when most of exhausted society followed the Prince of Wales to Brighton.

Mr John Rainbird, butler of Number 67, stood out on the step and gloomily surveyed the Stygian scene. Life had looked so promising last Season. Their tenants had been so generous that Rainbird had planned to buy a small pub in Highgate and take his 'family' – the rest of the staff – with him. But while they had all been away from the house at Fiona Sinclair's wedding, their money had been stolen. All suspected Jonas Palmer, but they had no proof. So instead of glorious, independent freedom, they were all still chained to the town house – as chained as the iron dogs on the steps at Rainbird's feet.

The long wars with Napoleon raged on, a quartern loaf cost one shilling and ninepence, and the starving poor died daily in the streets. The servants, who were paid only enough to keep body and soul together, foraged for what they could. Only that morning, Angus MacGregor, the Highland cook, had set out to walk to the country beyond Kensington to search for firewood; Mrs Middleton, the housekeeper, genteel daughter of a curate, had plucked up her courage and gone to Covent Garden to see what vegetables she could find; and little Lizzie, the between-stairs-cum-scullery maid, was at the baker's to see if she could purchase a loaf of stale bread.

The chambermaid, Jenny, and housemaid, Alice, were indoors, dismally cleaning and polishing the empty rooms, for Jonas Palmer delighted in surprise visits and would walk from room to room wearing a pair of white cotton gloves with which to run over every ledge to make sure there was not even one speck of dust.

Rainbird sighed and shivered. Joseph, the tall footman, minced up the area steps and came to stand beside him. The two men looked into the shifting fog in silence. Joseph was tall, fair, and good-looking, his round blue eyes fringed with fair skimpy lashes that were his private despair. Rainbird was much shorter than Joseph with a sinewy acrobat's body and a comedian's face. He had a pair of clever, sparkling grey eyes, which usually shone with good humour but of late had been as dull and sad as the weather.

One large flake of snow spiralled down and landed on Joseph's nose. He brushed it away. 'A pox on this weather,' he said, his voice high and affected. 'It does give a fellow the blue devils.'

'Perhaps you might not feel so bad if you stirred yourself to do something,' said Rainbird sharply. 'Have you cleaned the silver?'

'No,' said Joseph sulkily. 'Eh'm tired of cleaning the demned stuff.'

'Then do it now,' said Rainbird crossly. 'Remember you and I are in a worse position than the others should Palmer take against us.'

Both men had been dismissed from *tonnish* houses for crimes of which they were innocent. But they had been declared guilty, and Palmer always threatened to broadcast their misdemeanours should they not jump to his every bidding, which would mean that neither would have the hope of finding employment ever again.

It was perhaps this shared misfortune that made Rainbird tolerate the effeminate and often waspish footman. Rainbird was also perhaps the only person who saw the shrinking, sensitive creature under the affectations.

'Dave isn't doing nothing,' whined Joseph.

'Dave is cleaning out the chimneys.'

'So he should,' sneered Joseph, 'seeing as how it's the only trade he knows.'

Dave had been a chimney boy, rescued by Rainbird from a harsh master. Palmer was unaware of his existence. Dave was unofficially the pot boy.

'Go inside. You weary me, Joseph,' said Rainbird.

Joseph flounced off, and Rainbird turned his gaze back to the swirling fog.

Lizzie came scurrying out of the gloom, her pattens clack-clacking on the stones. She was carrying something wrapped in a shawl.

To Rainbird's surprise, she ignored his greeting and plunged down the area steps like an animal fleeing to its burrow.

He nimbly ran down after her. Lizzie went through into the servants' hall, whatever it was she held in her shawl cradled against her breast like a baby.

'What have you there?' demanded Rainbird.

Fog lay in bands across the room, which was dimly lit by one evil-smelling tallow candle in the centre of the table. Lizzie silently unwrapped her shawl, took out a large crusty loaf, and put it on the table. Then she sat with her head bowed.

Rainbird walked forward and picked up the loaf. 'This is fresh, Lizzie,' he said. 'You only had a penny for a bit of stale bread. How did you come by this?'

Lizzie's eyes, enormous in her thin face, looked sorrowfully at the butler. Two large tears spilled over and cut two clean tracks through the fog-grime on her cheeks.

A sudden horrible thought struck Rainbird. 'You didn't, Lizzie. I mean, you didn't go with some man . . . ?'

'Worse than that,' shivered Lizzie.

Rainbird sat down. Alice and Jenny came into the kitchen demanding to know what the matter was, and Dave made them all jump by appearing down the chimney, covered in soot.

'I think I got abaht free bags full, Mr Rainbird,' he said cheerfully. 'I'll sell the soot this afternoon. What's up wiff our Liz?'

'Same as all of us,' drawled Joseph. 'Hunger.'

'Go on, Lizzie,' urged Rainbird. 'Tell us.'

The scullery maid brushed the tears away with her fingers. 'I went to Partridge's,' she said.

Rainbird gave a click of annoyance. 'What took you there? That's the most expensive baker in Mayfair.'

'Brown's in the market didn't have no stale bread. I thought a grand baker's might have some but folks wouldn't think of asking. So I went in.'

'And?' demanded Jenny, the chambermaid.

'And there was this fine lady with her two daughters.'

'Garn,' said Dave. 'Fine ladies don't buy their own bread out o' shops.'

'They was doing it for a sort of joke,' said Lizzie. '"See, my dears," said the grand lady, "you should never leave the shopping to servants all the time. One should occasionally go oneself to check that the prices tally with those in the housekeeper's books." One of the daughters stares at me and says, "But mama, one has to meet such common people like that dirty little servant girl." "It is not even *ladylike* to *notice* that class of person," says the mother. They all had baskets like Leghorn hats, flat and open and decorated with silk flowers. Partridge was charging two shillings and threepence for a large loaf and they bought six,' said Lizzie, her remembered awe drying her tears.

'They swep' past me. "Get out of my way, little peasant," says the mother, and, as she went past me, this loaf fell from her silly basket, and quick as a wink I caught it before it fell to the ground. They didn't wait. I ran after them as they were getting in their carridge and I says, "Please mum, you've dropped your loaf."

'"Oh, mama," says one of the girls, "don't touch it. She's probably got lice."

'"Then it will do the servants," says the mother, leaning out of the carridge window to take it from me.

'I found meself shouting, "Then *I'll* keep it," an' I wrapped it in my shawl and ran as hard as I could. They screamed, "Stop thief!" and hands grabbed at me out of the fog, but I darted into a doorway and hid there until the shouting died away. So here I am,' she ended miserably.

Rainbird took a deep breath. 'Lizzie, if they had caught you, you would have been hanged, or, at the very least, transported to the colonies.'

'I am in mortal sin,' whispered Lizzie.

'So you are,' crowed Joseph. 'That Pope o' yourn will damn you to hell.' Then he gasped as Jenny drove her sharp elbow into his solar plexus.

'I think God will forgive you,' said Rainbird, 'but whether he will forgive that woman and her daughters is another matter. Dry your tears, Lizzie. You must never do anything like that again.'

The tall and Junoesque Alice walked slowly round the table – everything Alice did was slow and languid. She put her arms around Lizzie and said, 'Don't cry. You be a *good* girl.'

Rainbird sighed. What was their life sinking to when even such as little Lizzie turned thief?

Slow, heavy steps on the stairs heralded the arrival of the housekeeper, Mrs Middleton, a tired anxious lady of uncertain years with a face like a frightened rabbit. She opened her huge reticule and triumphantly placed a large, moth-eaten-looking cabbage on the table.

'How much?' asked Rainbird.

'Nothing,' beamed Mrs Middleton.

'You bin stealin' as well?' asked Dave.

'Get back up that chimney and mind your manners,' said Rainbird severely. 'Now, Mrs Middleton, what happened?'

'It was a porter at Covent Garden,' smiled Mrs Middleton, taking off her enormous bonnet, which looked like a coal scuttle. 'He dropped it and I picked it up and went after him. "Here, my good man," I said. "Oo d'ye think yer callin' *goodman*?" he says. "You can take that there cabbidge and . . ."' Mrs Middleton turned pink. 'I did not understand the rest of what he said, but he looked so violent that I said, "Thank you", and put the cabbage in my reticule. What did Dave mean about stealing as well?'

Joseph opened his mouth and then shut it again as Rainbird glared at him.

'Hurry up and finish those chimneys,' called Rainbird to Dave. 'Angus MacGregor has gone into the country for firewood so mayhap we'll have some heat this evening.'

'There's soot everywhere!' screamed Mrs Middleton. 'Alice, why are you hugging that useless maid? Lizzie, start scrubbing out this hall and when you've finished, get to work in the kitchen.'

'Here's MacGregor,' tittered Joseph, 'sounding like the whole of Prince Charles's rabble retreating from Derby.'

They all trooped into the kitchen where the Highland cook was just swinging a large sack down from his shoulder.

'Snowing hard,' he grunted.

'Blood!' screamed dark-haired Jenny. 'There's blood dripping from that sack!'

'What have you got there?' demanded Rainbird.

'A deer,' said the cook cheerfully. 'A wee bit cratur. Venison tonight.'

'You've been poaching on some lord's estate,' accused Rainbird.

'No,' said the red-haired cook laconically, jerking open the string that held the sack. 'It's a young 'un. I got it in the Green Park.'

'The King's deer,' whispered Rainbird. 'You great fool. They'll hang us all.'

'It was there for the asking,' said the unrepentant cook. 'I was that low in spirits for ah hud a great bag of firewood and I put it down to rest on the long road back and some blackguard stole it and ran off into the fog.' Rainbird had carried in one tallow candle when he had heard Angus MacGregor's arrival. In its dim circle of golden light, the faces of the servants were as white as paper. 'Don't look sae feart,' went on the cook crossly. 'I was coming through the park and there was this little deer with a broke leg and next to death wi' the cold. I took out ma knife and slit its throat. I had a spare sack wi' me so I hefted it up and ran here.'

He cocked his head to one side and they all stiffened as the heavy tread of marching feet sounded up in Clarges Street outside.

'And dripping blood all the way,' said Rainbird, panic-stricken. 'You've brought the whole militia down on us. The volunteers drill in the parks every day . . .'

'Tie it on my back,' said Dave. 'Quick!'

'Why . . . ?' began Rainbird.

'Tie it on,' screamed Dave. Heavy steps began to descend outside. While Angus MacGregor quickly lashed the deer onto the pot boy's back, while Alice and Jenny frantically scrubbed at the blood stains on the floor, there came a loud, imperative knock at the door.

'Open in the King's name!' called a harsh voice.

Dave scrambled into the empty kitchen grate with the deer on his back. He seized the first of the iron rungs that had been placed inside the chimney for the sweep's climbing boys. 'Push me up,' he hissed to MacGregor.

Mrs Middleton had often bemoaned the old-fashioned open range with its wide chimney, but now she thanked God feverishly for Jonas Palmer's parsimony.

Rainbird opened the door. A tall captain with snow glistening on his scarlet regimentals pushed his way into the kitchen. With him came a sergeant, a trooper, and a Bow Street Runner.

'Stay outside, the rest of you, until you are called,' shouted the captain over his shoulder.

'What can I do for you?' asked Rainbird.

'Where is your master?' demanded the captain.

'My master,' said Rainbird, 'is the Duke of Pelham. He is at Oxford University. In the meantime, I am in charge here.'

'Name?'

'Mr John Rainbird.'

The captain jerked his head, and his sergeant held up a lanthorn next to the butler's face. The captain studied the butler from head to foot. Rainbird was wearing the livery bought for him by the previous tenant – black tail coat, white waistcoat, black silk knee breeches, white stockings, and buckled shoes.

'It's like this,' said the captain, a reluctant tinge of respect creeping into his voice. 'Some female reports she's seen a man kill a deer in the Green Park. Sure enough, there was blood on the snow. We followed the trail o' blood and it led right here. So we're going to search this house from attic to cellar.'

'Fustian,' snorted Rainbird. 'I am not a thief, sirrah.'

'Mayhap. But one o' you is. How do you explain that trail o' blood?'

'I have no idea,' said Rainbird, very stiffly on his stiffs.

There came a faint curse from inside the chimney.

'Who's there?' called the captain sharply.

'It's only the climbing boy,' said MacGregor.

'Scotch, hey?' said the captain suspiciously. The Scots unless they were of the upper class were still regarded with distrust and suspicion and often spat on in the street. Were they not savage foreigners who descended on the south in hordes and took jobs away from decent Englishmen? He glanced downward at MacGregor's shoes, his eyes narrowing at the traces of mud and melting snow.

'I'll just take a look up that chimney,' he said.

'Help!' came a wail from the scullery. 'Oh . . . I am *dying*.'

'It's Lizzie!' cried Rainbird. He made a move to the scullery door, but, as he did so, the door swung open and Lizzie staggered over the threshold. Bright blood spurted from a vein in her wrist and her eyes were wild with fear.

'Gad's 'Oonds!' cried the officer.

Rainbird snatched out his handkerchief, seized a wooden spoon, and twisted a tourniquet around the top of Lizzie's arm. 'What happened, girl?' he demanded, forgetting their peril in this new fright.

'I was in the Green Park,' whispered Lizzie through white lips, 'and I slipped and fell in the snow and cut my wrist on a broken wine bottle.'

'We will get her to St George's Hospital,' said Alice, coming forward into the light. 'You will help us, Captain.' She said it as a statement, not as a request. The captain looked at the golden wings of Alice's hair shining under her crisp cap, at the slow rise and fall of her beautiful bosom, at the creamy skin of her face, and the wide cerulean blue of her eyes.

The deer was forgotten. Orders were barked out. A hackney carriage was brought to the door outside. Rainbird picked Lizzie's frail body up in his arms, cursing softly under his breath as he carried her up the stairs.

Joseph followed, digging his hand in the pocket of his livery. He brought out a lace and cambric handkerchief and looked at it longingly. It was his dearest treasure. Then he leant over Lizzie where she lay back in a corner of the hackney and held out the handkerchief. 'For you, Lizzie,' he said in a low voice. He leaned forward and kissed her thin, white cheek.

Now Lizzie had harboured a secret love for the tall footman since the first day she had started work at Number 67. 'Thank you, Mr Joseph,' she whispered, taking the handkerchief and putting it in her bosom.

The captain was to say long afterwards that he had never seen such a brave servant girl. She had smiled dreamily while a surgeon at St George's had stitched her wound. So transfigured by happiness did she look that an old lady at the hospital fell to her knees in awe, thinking Lizzie was a dying girl on the threshold of heaven.

The snow was falling thick and fast as they put Lizzie to bed in one of the best bedrooms upstairs. Palmer would not venture out on such a night, and Lizzie, who had cut her own wrist to save them all, must have only the best.

Then a terrified Dave, who had not the faintest

idea of what had been going on, had to be rescued from the chimney. He was sobbing with fatigue, having hung onto the rungs with the weight of the carcase on his back for some two hours.

'You should be ashamed of yourself, Angus,' said Rainbird severely to the cook. 'Two children nigh dead over your folly.'

'Aye, weel, you'll sing a different tune when ye've all got a bit of roast venison inside,' said the unrepentant cook, untying the deer from Dave's back.

'Lizzie saved us all,' said Mrs Middleton. 'God bless her.'

Rainbird sighed wearily as the snow whispered at the area windows, which were set high up in the wall. 'It is so cold,' he said. 'We have nothing to make a fire, Angus. Do you expect us to eat that animal raw?'

'I cannae dae everything,' said the cook sulkily.

'They had coal delivered next door today,' said Dave, recovering from all his shocks with his usual resilience. 'Sacks and sacks o' it, straight dahn the coal 'ole in big shiny lumps.'

Rainbird's eyes sharpened. 'Lizzie must have heat,' he said. '*We* must have heat.' He sat for a few moments in brooding silence. He looked round at the servants who, with the exception of Lizzie, were all sitting about, made listless by the intense cold.

'No one must ever steal anything again,' he said, 'but there is no harm in *borrowing*. Now, as we were returning from the hospital you must have noticed that Lord Charteris next door was leaving for the country with all his staff. That means the house is empty.'

'That's right,' said Joseph, looking at the butler curiously. 'Luke told me t'other day they was all leaving.' Luke was the Charterises' first footman.

'Down in our cellar,' said Rainbird dreamily, 'there is a pick and a shovel.' He stood up, a slow grin curling his mobile mouth. 'Strip off, Joseph, my boy. Tonight, we mine for coal!'

'Me 'ands,' wailed Joseph, reverting to that Cockney whine of his that was normally covered by a thin layer of affected gentility.

'Wear gloves, you Jessamy,' said Rainbird. 'To work!'

Lizzie in the bedroom upstairs drifted in and out of sleep. At one point she tried to struggle out of bed because there were great hammerings and thumps reverberating through the house, and she thought the militia had come back. But she was too exhausted to make much of an effort and soon fell back into an uneasy doze.

She awoke sometime during the evening. A fire was crackling on the hearth, throwing a dancing rosy glow up to the ceiling. Warmth crept through her body, and she wondered dreamily where they had found the coal. Then, all at once, Joseph was bending over her, stripped to the waist and black with coal dust.

'You still got my kerchief, Lizzie?' he whispered.

'Yes, Joseph,' said Lizzie mistily. 'I'll never part with it.'

Joseph's face fell. 'Mr Joseph to you, minx,' he grumbled, slouching away.

He joined the rest of the black and weary servants in the hall.

'What's this?' he cried. 'Only bread and water?'

'You'll get something later,' said MacGregor. 'I'm going to fry the liver. But the beast's got to be hung.'

Rainbird looked down the table at the weary, dejected faces.

'Be of good cheer,' he said. 'I do not think the Good Lord above meant us to starve in Mayfair. Somewhere, right at this moment, someone is planning to take this house. I know it. I *feel* it.'

But the wry twist at his mouth and the weary sadness in his eyes gave the lie to his optimism.

TWO

It's all very well to be handsome and tall,
Which certainly makes you look well at a ball:
It's all very well to be clever and witty,
But if you are poor, why it's only a pity.

ARTHUR HUGH CLOUGH, *SPECTATOR AB EXTRA*

In a small village twelve miles outside Brighton lived a small, plain girl who did not know yet that she was to stay at Number 67 Clarges Street and change the fortunes of the staff. She was only eighteen years of age and had not yet put her hair up. Her name was Jane Hart, daughter of a retired sea captain.

At the very moment that Dave was frantically climbing up the chimney with the deer, as brave little Lizzie was slashing her wrist in the scullery, Jane Hart was sitting at the window of her bedroom, a romance lying on her lap, and gazing unseeingly out at the white mist rolling over the Sussex downs.

Her sister, Euphemia, often laughingly referred

to her as Plain Jane. For Jane was as brown-skinned as her sister was fair, as small as Euphemia was tall, and as shy as her sister was bold. Although Jane naturally did not like to be called plain, she had to admit that no young lady she had ever met was as beautiful as Euphemia, and, therefore, it was understandable that anyone would pale before such beauty.

Euphemia was nineteen and a fashionable goddess. Her hair was naturally curly and of a rich brown. Her pale skin was without blemish and her large brown eyes, liquid and full. She had a small straight nose and a tiny mouth, the upper lip being larger than the lower.

Jane had tough, coarse, gypsy hair that frizzed in damp weather. Her thin face was golden-brown, her mouth was large and generous, and, alas, her nose was decidedly snub.

Her large eyes were hazel and fringed with sooty lashes. Her uncle, Mr Hardwicke, had once praised the beauty of Jane's eyes, but Mrs Hart, Jane's mother, had sniffed and said Jane's bad skin-colouring ruined any possibility of beauty.

Mrs Hart, who had once been a great beauty, had disappointed her parents by marrying a sea captain. Jane had often heard her father described as being dashing and handsome in his youth, but the captain was now a sullen, morose, lantern-jawed man, nagged by his wife. It was hard to think he had ever been young.

Mrs Hart had a great deal of money of her own.

She had nagged her husband until he had reluctantly resigned his command right after the Battle of Trafalgar in 1805 and settled into bitter retirement.

The family, considering the amount of Mrs Hart's wealth, could have lived in more comfortable circumstances. But Mrs Hart was penny-pinching to a fault and so they were confined to a damp barracks of a mansion in an undistinguished village with few diversions. Practically their only caller was Lady Doyle, relict of an Irish peer, who claimed to know every society figure of note in London. Mrs Hart considered Lady Doyle good *ton.*

Mrs Hart's parsimony did not run to Euphemia's dowry, which was large. No dowry had even been discussed when it came to Jane, and sometimes Jane dismally thought spinsterhood lay in front of her for, without money, there was little hope of marriage.

Lady Doyle was at that moment belowstairs being entertained to tea. Jane sighed. Her mother could not understand anyone disliking so grand a personage as Lady Doyle and would already be resenting Jane's absence.

Jane stood up, gathering up the long skirts of her gown – a hand-me-down from Euphemia – and reluctantly made her way downstairs. On the half-landing was a long thin window. As Jane looked up at it she could see large feathery flakes of snow beginning to fall. Lady Doyle would no doubt cut short her visit so that she might travel to her home at the other end of the village, Upper Patchett, before the weather grew worse.

A murmur of voices from the drawing room filtered out through the panels of the thick oak door. Jane pushed open the door and walked in. Her father was sitting at one side of the fire, moodily cracking his knuckles and staring into the flames. On the other side, with a fire screen on a long pole raised to shield her face, was Lady Doyle.

She had a long, drooping, curved face, rather like the reflection of a face in a spoon. She still wore old-fashioned panniered skirts and powdered hair. Only one small rebellious tendril showed that her hair was powdered, for the rest was covered by a starched frilled cap, with a broad-brimmed beaver hat on top of that. Her large teeth were very white and strong, but broken in places, making them look like a new castle's ramparts that have been recently shelled. The firelight flickered on the gold embroidery of her velvet gown and sparkled on the heavy rings on her long bony fingers.

Mrs Hart turned as Jane entered the room and threw her daughter a quick disapproving frown. Jane's mother's beauty hung about her like a pale ghost. There was something in the grace of her movements and the pout of her lips that showed she had once been a diamond of the first water. But too much use of *blanc* with a lead base had pitted her skin and disappointment had soured her expression. Although she would not admit it, her mouth had once been as generous as Jane's, but years of primming it up to reduce it to a fashionable size had left her with the odd appearance of always being on the point of whistling, and she had a thin network of wrinkles radiating out from her lips.

Euphemia glanced at her little sister with indifference. Then she returned to practising her Attitude, which was of Dreaming Beauty. This involved turning her eyes up to the ceiling while resting the tip of her forefinger on her cheek.

Jane sat down quietly in a corner and folded her hands meekly in her lap. With any luck, she might escape Lady Doyle's malicious attention. But Lady Doyle's next words fell like a heavy stone into the silence that had fallen when Jane had entered the room.

'I see there's a town house to rent in Clarges Street for the Season. A prodigious low rent. I was thinking, it's such a shame a beauty like Euphemia who could marry a duke should waste her looks upon the country air.'

Jane remembered the snow. 'It is beginning to snow heavily,' she ventured, but neither Euphemia nor her mother paid her the slightest heed. Euphemia's large eyes were now fastened on Lady Doyle's unlovely face with an expression of greedy hope. Mrs Hart stood like a statue, the silver teapot in her hand. 'How much?' she asked.

'Eighty pounds, and that includes furnishings and trained staff.'

'Clarges Street,' mused Mrs Hart. 'A fine address.

That runs between Piccadilly and Curzon Street, does it not?'

Lady Doyle nodded. 'In the centre of everything,' she said, helping herself to the last slice of seed cake. 'I have told you before,' she went on, her voice muffled with cake, 'that with my connections, you could secure a great match for Euphemia.'

Mr Hart got up and left the room. No one noticed him leave, except Jane.

'I am not a rich woman, and yet . . .' Mrs Hart bent over the tea table to replace the pot and the firelight winked and sparkled on the heavy diamond pendant about her neck.

'You have heard me speak of Sally, Lady Jersey?' demanded Lady Doyle.

'Yes, indeed.'

'A dear friend. We are as close as inkle weavers. Lady Jersey has only to hear from me and she will arrange vouchers for Euphemia.'

'To Almack's?' breathed Euphemia.

'To Almack's,' confirmed Lady Doyle.

Almack's, that temple of society, held assemblies every Wednesday throughout the Season. To attend Almack's was to be In.

'There must be something up with this house,' said Mrs Hart cautiously. 'Eighty pounds! And servants!'

'It could be a printing error,' admitted Lady Doyle, 'but nothing ventured, nothing gained, as my dear husband used to say.'

'We do not need town servants,' said Mrs Hart. 'I do not want mine left here, eating their heads off.'

'But the servants in Mayfair come with the house,' pointed out Lady Doyle. 'And,' she added, 'you could rent *this* house to some genteel family desirous of sea breezes.' Twelve miles away, the sullen sea rolled against the pebbly beach of Brighton, but that was a mere bagatelle.

'I have hesitated to incur the expense of a Season,' said Mrs Hart while her busy mind was turning over the possibilities of gaining a profitable rent for her home. 'The thing that held me back was lack of connections.'

'But you have *my* connections,' pointed out Lady Doyle. 'Do I not know the Countess Lieven and Mr Brummell himself . . . dear George, who calls me "his darling Harry"?' Then she gave a genteel cough and brushed cake crumbs from the panniers of her gown. 'She is going to get money out of mama somehow,' thought Jane, who knew that cough of old. It always presaged some delicate request for contributions to this or that charity. Jane sometimes wondered if the money did not go into Lady Doyle's reticule and stay there.

'Of course,' said Lady Doyle with a wide smile, 'it *does* incur a certain leetle expense. Our dear members of the *ton* like to be thanked with tasteful gifts. However, if you will leave the choosing of such items to me, for I know the tastes of each one, and furnish me with the money, I will despatch them with the carrier – with one of your cards in each one.'

Mrs Hart winced, but the fires of ambition had

been lit in her breast. 'I will furnish you with any amount you think necessary,' she said, with a look of pain on her faded features as if contemplating an amputation.

Lady Doyle's pale eye moved from the now empty cake plate to the window where large snow flakes were crowding thick and fast against the glass. 'Goodness! I must leave,' she said. 'Pray ring for my carriage. You will find, Mrs Hart, that any money you give me for gifts will be well spent. It is not as if you have to go to any expense for Jane. *She* will *never* take.'

Euphemia gave her charming, rippling laugh and glanced sideways at Jane, and then frowned. For there was no hurt look on Jane's face.

Jane was lost in a dream.

For by simply going to London, she might see *him* again.

The fact that *he* might be married after eight long years never crossed her mind.

She had first seen Beau Tregarthan in the summer of 1800 when she was ten years old and had dreamed of him ever since.

The normally sleepy village of Upper Patchett had been alive with gossip about the great prize fight that was to be held on the downs. Sir Bartholomew Anstey was putting his man, Jack Death, into the ring against an unknown contender, promised and sponsored by Beau Tregarthan. The odds were running ten to one in Jack Death's favour, although many would have loved to see the most savage bruiser of the English boxing scene get his comeuppance. He had beaten his last opponent to death. But very few wanted to stake money on an unknown.

Bored with endless lessons given by a governess who was strict towards herself and dotingly lenient towards Euphemia, Jane longed for adventure. Finally, on the day of the prize fight, she slipped from the house with one of her father's old beaver hats down about her ears and a muffler up to her eyes. She wore one of her father's old coats, which trailed on the ground at her heels. She hoped anyone seeing her would take her for some village boy.

She reached the outer edge of the crowd that had gathered that hot August day on the downs. For several minutes, she stared despairingly at the row of masculine backs blocking her view. Then retreating up the slope of the downs, she saw a small tree and, hampered by her heavy coat, she managed to climb it with difficulty.

The ring was in the middle of a hollow, the slope of the downs all about forming a natural amphitheatre. In the very middle stood the Master of the Ring, Gentleman Jackson. Jane fished out her father's telescope from one capacious pocket and put it in her eye. Jackson was a splendid figure in a scarlet coat worked with gold at the button-holes, a white stock, a looped hat with a broad black band, buff knee breeches, white silk stockings, and paste buckles. He had a hard, high-boned face and piercing eyes, in all a magnificent figure with those splendid 'balustrade' calves that had helped him to be the finest runner and jumper in England as well as the most formidable pugilist.

Around the edge of the ring stood the beaters-off in their high white hats. Their job was to wield their whips and stop any spectator setting foot in the ring.

A cheer went up as a white hat with scarlet ribbons sailed into the ring. Jack Death had arrived, and, amid a roar from the crowd, he followed his hat into the ring. His chest was bare, and he wore a pair of white calico drawers, white silk stockings, and running shoes. Round his waist was a scarlet sash, and dainty scarlet ribbons fluttered at his knees. He was broad-chested and swarthy. There was something almost ape-like about his long slingy arms and his thrusting jaw.

Two men below the tree in which Jane crouched were becoming anxious that the fight might not take place. 'Lord Tregarthan's man has not arrived and there's only five minutes to go,' said one. The crowd craned their necks this way and that. Soon, there was only a minute left.

Then a jaunty black beaver hat sailed into the ring. The cheer that followed its appearance was so loud, so exuberant, that Jane clung onto the branch on which she was lying, afraid it might throw her off her perch like some great wave.

'Who's his man?' asked the man below her.

''Fore George,' cried his companion, 'it's Tregarthan himself.'

Jane peered down her telescope and then held her breath. The cheers of the crowd had become mixed with laughter. A London exquisite had strolled into the ring. Beau Tregarthan himself. He drew off his gloves and tossed them to a stocky man, who was fussing about him. Gentleman Jackson appeared to be remonstrating with Lord Tregarthan, but the beau just smiled and stripped off his coat, his waistcoat, and his shirt. Then he turned and faced his opponent.

The laughter died and there was a murmur of admiration. Jane screwed the telescope so hard into her eye that she carried a red mark around it for all of the next day.

The beau stood in the middle of the ring, stripped to the waist. His skin was white and fine. When he moved, the light of the sun caught the beautiful liquid rippling of his muscles.

'Strips well,' murmured the man below Jane. 'How stand the odds?'

'Seven to one now,' grunted his companion.

The beau waved to the crowd. His hair gleamed guinea-gold. He had a high-nosed handsome profile. A great silence fell on the crowd as Gentleman Jackson held up his hands. His stentorian voice carried far over the downs in the still air. There was not even a breath of wind.

'Gentlemen!' cried Jackson. 'Sir Bartholomew Anstey's nominee is Jack Death, fighting at thirteen-eight, and Lord Tregarthan's nominee is . . . Lord Tregarthan, fighting at eleven stone-three. No person can be allowed at the inner ropes save the referee and time-keeper. All ready?'

'Too light,' complained the voice below. 'Shan't bet on Tregarthan. Too light. Corinthian though he is, Jack Death'll kill him.'

'No! He cannot!' squeaked Jane in alarm. She lost her grip and fell out of the tree at the feet of the two men below.

Her hat tumbled from her head.

One of the men turned out to be Mr Wright, the village blacksmith.

'*Miss Jane!*' he exclaimed. 'Off along home with you.'

'Don't tell my mother,' gasped Jane. 'Oh, *please*, Mr Wright.'

'Reckon I won't,' said the blacksmith who had no love for the cheese-paring Mrs Hart. 'But I will, mark you, if you don't get out o' here sharpish.'

Suddenly horrified at what would happen to her should anyone else spot her and tell her mother, Jane crammed her hat down on her eyes and ran all the way home. Although she managed to enter the house unobserved, she received a stern dressing-down from her governess for having missed her lessons in the schoolroom. But Jane escaped the birch beating she usually received for any misdemeanour by bursting into overwrought tears.

Alarmed, and sure she had some dangerous infection, the governess rushed to tell Mrs Hart – for she had never known Jane cry before. Jane was promptly put to bed. The doctor, hurriedly summoned, diagnosed brain fever caused by an excess of lessons, for he had once made advances to the governess and had had them rejected. His prescription was that Jane should spend six weeks away from her books.

Normally this would have delighted Jane, but all that day she tossed and turned, imagining the beautiful Lord Tregarthan being beaten to a pulp. When the maid came in with Jane's bedtime glass of hot milk, Jane could bear the suspense no longer. Struggling up against the pillows, she asked as casually as she could. 'What was the outcome of the prize fight?'

'Young ladies should not know about such things,' said the maid repressively, placing the glass of milk by the bedside and heading for the door.

'Oh, *Martha*,' pleaded Jane.

Martha suddenly grinned and came and sat on the bed. 'Well, Miss Jane, you never did! 'Tis said Lord Tregarthan himself went into the ring against Jack Death and he floored him in the fifteenth round. Jack Death was bleeding so hard about the face he could not see and my lord did not even have a mark on him. Seems my lord's man was bedded with the fever the night before so my lord decided to fight himself. How they cheered him!'

Jane burst into tears of relief.

'Quiet,' hissed Martha, looking anxiously at the door. 'You'll get me into trouble. You should never have asked me.'

She waited anxiously until Jane gulped and smiled and said, 'I shall do very well now, Martha.'

During that night, Jane decided to marry Beau Tregarthan.

As she grew older and plainer, she knew she could never hope to attract the attentions of such a god. But if she hoped and hoped and waited and waited and prayed very hard, perhaps the fates might allow her one glimpse of him – just one more time.

THREE

There's no use in being young without being beautiful, and no use in being beautiful without being young.

LA ROCHEFOUCAULD, *MAXIMS*

The arrival of Joseph Palmer at Number 67 Clarges Street was most unexpected. Neither Rainbird nor any of the other servants had expected him to venture out in such weather.

The snow had fallen steadily for days and then had frozen hard, squeaking beneath the Londoners' feet as they scurried through the cold. A biting north-easter had blown the fog away. Blocks of ice churned about the steely waters of the Thames.

MacGregor fortunately had espied the stocky figure of the agent in Bolton Row and had rushed to warn the others of his impending arrival. The blazing kitchen fire was doused with a bucket of water and the back door was opened to chill the servants' hall and kitchen. Palmer knew they had not any money for coal and would immediately demand to know where they had found it.

Lizzie, almost completely recovered, had been moved out of the upstairs bedroom, but still Alice and Jenny flew upstairs to make sure there was not the slightest trace of her recent occupation.

The wind had abruptly died and a pale disk of a sun was moving down the sky as Jonas Palmer stood on the step and scraped the mud and snow from his boots on the iron scraper set into the wall of the house. He performed a brisk tattoo on the brass knocker and then fidgeted impatiently on the step while the pattering of hastening feet crossed and recrossed the hall inside.

At last Rainbird opened the door. He did not look in the least surprised to see Palmer, and the agent crossly guessed that they had been forewarned of his arrival. Palmer stumped past the butler and went into the front parlour on the ground floor. A dim white light shone through the frost flowers on the window, and the room was as cold as the grave.

'The windows will soon be cracking with frost if you don't fire the house properly,' said Palmer sourly. He was a heavy-set man who looked like a farmer with his great coarse red face. There were tufts of grey hair sprouting from each nostril and adorning his cheeks.

'You did not give us any money for fuel, and sea coal is dear,' pointed out Rainbird.

Palmer stared at the floor.

'Should any tenant come to inspect the premises first,' pursued Rainbird, 'they might not wish to take such a cold house.'

'Had a hard winter, heh?' grinned Palmer.

'Like everyone else.'

'We'll see about getting you coal, for the house has been let.'

Rainbird's face remained impassive.

'It's a member of the gentry,' said Palmer. 'A Captain Hart, his wife and two daughters. But there's a problem of sleeping space.'

'There is enough,' said Rainbird. There was a bedroom at the back of the dining room on the first floor and two bedrooms on the second.

'Mrs Hart is bringing a fancy French lady's maid and wishes her to have a room separate from the common servants.'

'Then it can't be done,' said Rainbird, surprised, 'unless the daughters share a room and give the other on the second floor to the maid. I gather Mr and Mrs Hart will wish to take the large bedroom next to the dining room.'

'Seems the daughters must have a room apiece,' said the agent. 'So Mrs Middleton will have to give up her parlour.'

Mrs Middleton, the housekeeper, had a small cosy parlour on a half-landing on the kitchen stairs. It was her pride and joy, but Rainbird knew that not one of them was in a position to protest. They all desperately needed a tenant for the Season.

'And the Harts' is the only offer?' he asked.

'The only one that I'm taking,' said the agent. 'They're paying in advance.'

Mrs Hart had been advised to do this by Lady

Doyle in case the house should prove to be £800 instead of £80. 'Pay in advance,' Lady Doyle had urged, 'and get the lease letters so that if they have made a mistake, they cannot go back on it.'

'Very well,' said Rainbird. 'I shall tell Mrs Middleton to prepare the parlour for the French maid.'

'And none of your womanizing tricks with the maid,' said Palmer.

'I do not go in for womanizing.'

'Ho, no? You what was dismissed from Lord Trumpington's household for bedding his wife?'

'The only crime there was that I was found out,' said Rainbird stiffly.

He had been a young footman at the time and had been well and truly seduced by Lady Trumpington, but her husband had cried rape and Rainbird was glad to escape with only the punishment of a bad reference. Still, the scandal clung to him wherever he went.

''Tis monstrous cold. Is there no tea?' asked Palmer.

'Alice will be along directly,' said Rainbird, ringing the bell. He was torn between elation at the idea of having a tenant and worry over Mrs Middleton's distress when she found out she had to give up her parlour.

Because Palmer surmised they had been warned of his coming, he did not inspect the premises – which was just as well because the servants' hall and the kitchen were both still suspiciously warm.

Rainbird was glad to see him go after an hour of instructions. He had not liked the way Palmer's pig-like eyes had rested on Alice's bosom as the maid had bent over to deposit the tea tray on a low table.

To Rainbird's relief, Mrs Middleton stoically agreed to transform her parlour into a bedchamber for the lady's maid. It was not the giving up of her sanctum that disturbed her, she said, but that the Harts should have employed a *French* maid. What was the world coming to when English servants were not considered good enough? This foreigner would probably murder them all in their beds in the way that Napoleon's troops were murdering British men abroad. The French were savages. Everyone knew that!

But Rainbird, wise in the ways of the *ton*, pointed out that society still interlarded their conversation with bad French, slavishly copied French fashion, hired French chefs, and generally went on as if there were not a war raging across the Channel.

The new tenants were to arrive at the beginning of March and stay until the end of June. Surely a family who could indulge in the frivolity of a French maid would be open-handed and generous.

In the late afternoon, Lizzie asked permission to go out. The previous tenant, Miss Fiona, now the missing Countess of Harrington, had once urged Lizzie to eat raw vegetables and to take as much fresh air as possible, and Lizzie, pleased that her disfiguring spots had gone, still followed her advice.

Her wrist had healed, although she would carry the scar to the end of her days. As she walked towards the Green Park, her thoughts turned as they usually did to Joseph, the footman. Little did Lizzie know that the vain footman longed to be able to take his precious handkerchief back but could not steal it because Lizzie kept it under her gown, next to her heart. Lizzie wondered what the French maid would be like. What if Joseph fell in love with her?

The sun was setting and the trees in the park cast their long black shadows across the snow. Lizzie stood silently, thinking of Joseph, as the sun turned to red as it sank lower. The snow burned crimson, one glorious blazing sheet of rubies, and then slowly changed to grey with bluish tinges in the hollows.

Lizzie had come to Clarges Street from the orphanage. Her parents had died just after she was born and the servants in Clarges Street had become her adopted family.

She shivered as a sudden wind rattled the skeletal branches of the winter trees. As she turned about to head home, she saw a bundle lying near the edge of the reservoir. In the hope that someone might have dropped some firewood, she went closer – and then drew in a sharp breath of anguish. A mother and child lay half buried in the snow. The child was about three years old, its dead face turned to the darkening sky.

Frozen to death!

She swayed as she remembered the death of

Clara, daughter of the second tenants of Number 67. She, too, had been found dead on the edge of the reservoir. Lizzie stumbled away towards the cottage at the gates of the park where two elderly ladies kept the herd of cows that supplied fresh milk to Mayfair. She banged on the door. A tall old lady dressed in the style of Louis XV – high lace cap and gown of brocaded silk – opened the door.

'Please, mum,' gabbled Lizzie, 'there's a woman and child by the reservoir, and, oh, mum, they's dead . . . starved and froze.'

'Indeed,' said the lady. 'So inconsiderate. I will tell the rangers. You may go. Wait! Do you know who I am?'

Lizzie bobbed a curtsy. 'No, mum.'

'I,' said the lady, drawing herself up and looking down her long thin nose at Lizzie, 'am Mrs Searle.'

Lizzie looked blank.

'*I* am George Brummell's aunt.'

Even little Lizzie knew of George Brummell, that famous leader of fashion and close intimate of the Prince of Wales.

'Yes, you may stare,' went on Mrs Searle. 'I started him on his career. He was visiting me after he had just left Eton when the Prince of Wales called on me with the Marquess of Salisbury. The Prince was attracted by George's nice manners. He said, "As I find you intend to be a soldier I will give you a commission in my own regiment."'

All at once, remembering the face of the dead child, Lizzie burst into tears.

'Yes, you may well cry,' said Mrs Searle. 'I see you have guessed the tragedy of it. That wicked boy never came near me after I had set his feet on the road to success.'

Lizzie stumbled away, still crying.

Although the other servants tried to comfort her, they were slightly irritated by what they considered Lizzie's excessive sensibility. Certainly bodies in Mayfair were not so thick on the ground as they were in the less salubrious areas, but with dead bodies lying frozen all over London, and with dead bodies dangling from the gibbets, they privately thought Lizzie over-nice in her feelings, unsuitably so for a scullery maid.

Talk soon turned back to speculation on the character of the new tenants. The fire supplied by the coal taken from Lord Charteris's cellar warmed their bones.

Rainbird did not consider the taking of the coal as theft, for he could not tell the servants not to sin and then do it himself. He convinced himself that they had merely been *borrowing* the coal. Palmer had promised him a delivery. When it came they would put it back in the cellar next door.

Unaware of all the discussion and speculation going on about them, the future tenants of 67 Clarges Street prepared for the great exodus to London. Their own home had been let for the period of their absence to an elderly lady who proved to be a match for Mrs Hart when it came to beating down the price. But the fact that her home in Upper Patchett *had* been let, and at such short notice, did much to allay the pangs of being outwitted and outdone in Mrs Hart's breast.

Never for a moment did Jane think there would be any question of leaving her behind. But horror upon horrors, the old lady, a Mrs Blewett, who was to take their home expressed a wish to find a young female companion. Mrs Hart's eyes gleamed and she promptly suggested Jane – Jane who sat with her dreamworld of London and her possible meeting with Beau Tregarthan falling about her ears.

'It is not as if *you* were to make your come-out,' said Mrs Hart.

'I don't want an unwilling gel,' snapped Mrs Blewett, who had called to inspect the linen closet and assure herself the linen would not be damp. Mrs Blewett was fortunately not in need of sea breezes. Rather, she was fleeing from them as she lived in Brighton, and had let *her* home for a much larger sum than she was paying Mrs Hart.

'You will find Jane a congenial companion,' said Mrs Hart while her mind busily worked out the money she would save on Jane's gowns, what exactly she should charge for Jane's services, and that the whole arrangement would go a long way to defraying the expense of the smart new French maid. Lady Doyle had said that a French maid was *de rigueur*.

Euphemia looked worried. She teased and

tormented Jane, but, since she had no friends, she dreaded the thought of being launched into society with no one of her own age. Besides, Jane was an excellent foil for Euphemia's beauty.

'No,' said Mr Hart suddenly from his seat by the fire. 'Jane's going with us.'

All the ladies stared at him in surprise. Mrs Hart looked as amazed as if her wig stand had suddenly up and expressed an opinion. 'Mr Hart,' she said, casting an amused and tolerant look at Mrs Blewett as if to say 'these men', 'Jane will do very well with Mrs Blewett.'

Mr Hart rose to his feet. 'Jane's going,' he snapped. 'Let that be an end of the matter.' He strode from the room.

There was a long embarrassed silence. Mrs Hart fought to conceal her surprise at her usually silent husband's bid to assert himself. Then she gave a little shrug. 'That seems to be the way of it, Mrs Blewett. Mr Hart is very fond of our younger daughter.'

Mr Hart had previously shown little interest in either girl.

Jane let out a slow sigh of relief.

After Mrs Blewett had taken her leave and Mrs Hart fussed off to see what could possibly have driven her husband to voice an opinion for once in his life, Euphemia and Jane were left alone.

'I'm glad you are coming,' said Euphemia, giving her sister an impulsive hug. 'It is all rather terrifying, you know.' There was an almost comical expression of surprise on Euphemia's face. She had not been in the way of feeling in the slightest nervous when faced with social occasions before. In fact her bold manner at local assemblies usually verged on the indecent.

'The Season?' said Jane, round-eyed. 'Why, *you* have no need to be afraid, Euphemia. The gentlemen will fall over like ninepins when they see you.'

More in charity with her sister than she had been for a long while, Euphemia gave her another hug. 'Nonetheless,' she said, 'it is not as if I have any experience of the beau monde. I know I am beautiful, but I do not have any jewels. Mama is so clutch-fisted.'

'As to that,' said Jane, who studied the social columns, 'it is not at all the thing for debutantes to wear elaborate jewelry. Besides, you will marry a very rich man and have all the jewels you desire.'

'You must do everything in your power to help me,' said Euphemia. 'I do not want the gentlemen to take us in dislike because of that forthright tongue of yours. And papa is awkward in the saloon.'

'We have never seen papa in grand company, but he met many great men when he was serving in the navy so no doubt he knows how to go on better than any of us,' said Jane.

'Pooh! Stop sounding as if you know everything,' snapped Euphemia, a petulant look marring her beauty. 'Besides, mama will not waste time inviting *you* to balls and parties. She said so. She does not want to waste money on a wardrobe for you.'

'I think it is very unfair to be continually passed over,' said Jane in a low voice.

'It is not your fault you are so plain,' said Euphemia indifferently. 'Mama said to papa t'other day that she would take you to the local assemblies when I am puffed off. Squire Bascombe is said to be looking for a young bride.'

'Squire Bascombe is *fifty*, a widower, and has daughters older than I,' exclaimed Jane in horror.

Euphemia's unusual warmth towards her sister had now completely gone. 'You always were a depressing little thing,' she said, crossing to the glass to pat her curls.

Jane stormed out of the room. How lovely it would be to be able to put Euphemia's pretty nose out of joint . . . just once.

That night, after Jane had fallen asleep, her dreams took an odd turn. She dreamt she was walking down a London street with Euphemia. Beau Tregarthan drove past in his curricle. Now, in previous dreams, Euphemia had faded into a rosy mist while Beau Tregarthan's blue eyes gazed adoringly down into Jane's. But this time, he reined in his horses and sprang down from the curricle. He was no longer quite such a shadowy figure as in previous dreams, but very alive, very attractive, almost real. He advanced on the sisters, his eyes sparkling. He came to a stop in front of them. His blue eyes gazed with admiration on . . . Euphemia. It was Jane who felt herself fading away into the shadows beyond the circle of light that surrounded the pair.

She awoke with a start. The dream had been so vivid, so real – and so horribly possible. She climbed down from her bed and lit a candle from the rushlight in its pierced canister. Carrying the candle, she walked to the glass and stared at her reflection. Plain Jane stared back. With a muffled sob, she blew out the candle and plunged headlong into bed, burying herself under the blankets and trying to blot out that bright dream image of Euphemia with Beau Tregarthan.

FOUR

Like dragonflies the hansoms hover,
With jewelled eyes to catch the lover.
The streets are full of lights and loves,
Soft gowns and flutter of soiled doves.

The human moths about the light
Dash and cling close in dazed delight,
And burn and laugh, the world and wife
For this is London, this is life!

PAUL VERLAINE, *BALLAD OF LONDON*

The rigours of the winter were over at last as Lord Tregarthan sat at his desk and flicked through a pile of gilt-edged invitations. Behind him sat his friend, Mr Peter Nevill, a small, thin, angry man whom many of the *ton* considered an odd friend for the easy-going and elegant Beau Tregarthan to have.

Perhaps it was Mr Nevill's very lack of social graces and attitudes that attracted the over-courted and famous Beau, but then it was hard to tell what went on behind his handsome face and smiling blue eyes.

He had fought in the wars against Napoleon and had sold out after being invalided home. He had stated his intention of finding a wife at the Season, starting a family, and then taking himself off to the wars again.

Mr Nevill was a first-lieutenant in the navy, enjoying the first leave he had had in a long time. Both men had been to school together. Then, the larger Lord Tregarthan had been Mr Nevill's champion, and Mr Nevill still returned that championship with a fierce devotion.

The news that the famous beau was back on the London scene had gone round the drawing rooms and saloons of the elegant like wildfire . . . hence the small avalanche of invitations.

'Who is this Mrs Hart, 67 Clarges Street?' demanded Lord Tregarthan laconically. 'Keeps sending me cards.'

'Odd woman,' said Mr Nevill. 'Rumour has it she took that unlucky house because it was cheap.'

'Unlucky?'

'Yes. Duke of Pelham hanged himself there, one of the tenants found their daughter dead in the Green Park, another lot lost all their money or something. Ones who took it last year were a Mr Sinclair and his daughter, Fiona. *She* married the Marquess of Harrington and they went off on a long honeymoon and are now missing. Old Sinclair's said to have braved the whole of Boney's army to go looking for them. Unlucky house. This Hart female took it not knowing about its reputation.

Very pushing. Had to be set down. Embraced Sally Jersey in the Park, saying, "I am a friend of Lady Doyle." Lady Jersey pushed her away. Never heard of this Lady Doyle. Neither has anyone else.'

'Has she a marriageable daughter?'

'Ah, well, that's another thing. Daughter is a diamond of the first water. They're holding their first rout next week. Some going out of curiosity, but no one important.'

'It would amuse me to meet this daughter,' said Lord Tregarthan. 'Very few beauties around.'

'Family's bad *ton*,' said Mr Nevill. 'Well, that is, if the mother is anything to go by.'

'I would rather make up my own mind, Peter, as to whether anyone is bad *ton* or not. Society can be very cruel. Also, it would amuse me to see the inside of this unlucky house.'

'I'll go with you, if you like. But no one else of consequence will be there.'

'That should be refreshing.'

'But, o' course, if they know *you* are going, they'll all go.'

Lord Tregarthan smiled sweetly. 'Then let us not tell them, Peter. Let us see this haunted house in a modicum of peace and quiet.'

But, alas, for Lord Tregarthan's hopes of a quiet evening. Mrs Hart could not believe that Lady Doyle had been lying to her. After all, she had paid Lady Doyle quite a large sum of money to buy those gifts for the *ton*, and the present to Mr

Brummell of one snuff box had cost so much it had made Mrs Hart wince.

Although she was beginning to have a dim suspicion that Lady Doyle had pocketed the money without buying any gifts, Mrs Hart accosted the famous Mr Brummell when she had come across that arbiter of fashion walking along Pall Mall.

Had Mr Brummell not had a weakness for pretty females not yet turned twenty, and had Mrs Hart not been accompanied by Euphemia, then Mr Brummell would probably have given her the cut direct. But no sooner had his eyes fallen on Euphemia's enchanting face than he swept off his hat and made Mrs Hart his best bow in return to her almost over-familiar greeting.

Mrs Hart, elated, begged him to attend her rout, adding that she hoped he had received the snuff box she had sent him.

Now, by coincidence, the Duchess of Devonshire had sent Mr Brummell the present of a solid-gold snuff box inlaid with diamonds, which had arrived only that morning. But she had forgotten to put a card in with it. Mr Brummell, who had been wondering who had sent him such a magnificent present, smiled graciously on Mrs Hart, thanked her warmly, and said he would be delighted to attend her rout.

Flushed with triumph, Mrs Hart and Euphemia moved on. 'Everyone will come *now*,' said Mrs Hart. 'I am so relieved to find Lady Doyle actually sent him the snuff box in my name. I confess I was beginning to wonder if she were not, after all, the most consummate liar we have met.'

'Well, Jane always said she told fibs.'

'Pooh! What does Jane know?'

'Will Jane be attending the rout?' asked Euphemia.

'No, of course not. I have enough expense as it is without finding her a new gown.'

Euphemia bit her lip and glanced sideways at her mother. She did not want to admit to her mother that she was frightened of her forthcoming debut. But if Jane went, Euphemia would feel comfortably superior. She did not know that she often leaned on her younger sister's greater strength of character.

'I think it might be marked if your other daughter did not attend,' said Euphemia. 'Why not get that sly French maid to earn her keep for a change? She could alter one of my old silks to fit Jane.'

'Perhaps you have the right of it,' said Mrs Hart reluctantly. 'Servants are *such* a worry. Rainbird, the butler, seems very respectful and very well versed as to how to go on – although I must admit I was shocked when he pointed out to me I was expected to pay the staff extra wages. "Fustian," I said. But Rainbird told me that Lord Charteris, for example, always pays his servants extra for the Season and he hinted that upper servants do gossip and it might get about . . .'

Her voice trailed off into silence when she realized Euphemia was not listening.

The fact was that Rainbird had quickly learned how to manage Mrs Hart. At first, she had tried to make MacGregor produce gourmet meals on the smallest amount of money possible and had reduced Mrs Middleton to tears by quarrelling over pennies and halfpennies in the housekeeping books. Mrs Hart had been further incensed to learn that Palmer expected her to pay the new increased servants' tax, the new rate being fifteen shillings a year per male servant; females, like horses, being kept pretty much at the old tax level.

Rainbird had stepped in. Copying the most condescending manner of several of the worst butlers he had met, he set about putting Mrs Hart in her place. There would be Talk, said Rainbird firmly, if it got about that the food allowance and the servants' wages were not those of a *ton* household. And so he went on until life became more comfortable for the servants.

In fact, all the servants would have been happy had it not been for Felice, the French maid. Lizzie was as wary of her as if she had been some strange foreign animal like an orangutan. Yet Felice did not look in the least frightening, nor for that matter did she appear markedly foreign. She was a small neat woman of about thirty years. Everything about her seemed to be curved. Her eyelids curved, her mouth was curved in a perpetual half-smile, her dark-brown hair curved in two wings on either side of her face. She was round-shouldered and deep-bosomed. She had a tiny waist and small hands and feet. She said very little and seemed constantly employed. Although Mrs Hart had given instructions that the maid's meals were to be served to her in her room, Felice had chosen to join the other servants in the hall. It was not as if she particularly appeared to enjoy their company although her large black eyes gave nothing away. What made the females of the staff uneasy was the way she appeared to listen to every word as she bent her smooth head over a piece of sewing, for Felice's hands were busy even at mealtimes.

Although Alice, Jenny, Mrs Middleton, and even Lizzie could see nothing out of the way about her, Joseph deferred to her, MacGregor gave her the best cuts of meat, and even Dave ran her errands. Rainbird's twinkling, intelligent eyes softened as they watched her.

She was like a cat, thought Lizzie, a smooth, sleek, little cat. Joseph shows off to her the whole time, thought Lizzie gloomily, and has not a word to say to me.

Although Lizzie knew Joseph quite well, love had blinded her to the footman's extreme preoccupation with class and rank. The only female servants he considered his equal were governesses and lady's maids.

Felice could not be drawn to give any view on the war with the French. She admitted to having been previously employed by a Mrs Swan, a friend of Lady Doyle. But she never spoke about her parents, her background, or how she came over from France.

Lizzie decided that what was most upsetting about Felice was that she always seemed to be laughing inwardly at some private joke. Mrs Hart was a hard mistress and Felice had very little free time; what she had was taken up with sewing, but she never complained, never lost her temper, and never said very much.

The evening before the rout, the exhausted servants sat down to a late supper. Rainbird and Joseph had been moving furniture down into the cellars all day to leave the maximum amount of space for the guests. A rout was a peculiar affair. There were never any cards or dancing or music or refreshments: simply one huge mass of people congregated in one house, jostling and fighting their way in and then jostling and fighting their way out. Very few remained above half an hour.

Rainbird and Joseph were not only exhausted from heaving about the furniture but also from replacing Lord Charteris's coal and rebricking up the cellar wall.

'I don't suppose poor little Miss Jane will be allowed to go,' said Mrs Middleton, her great white cap casting a shadow over her face. 'They don't take her anywhere nor let her put her hair up. That Miss Euphemia calls her Plain Jane, but it is my considered opinion that Miss Jane would do very well with a bit of town bronze.'

Felice shook out the folds of burgundy silk on her lap. 'Miss Jane will look very well tomorrow evening, I think,' she volunteered.

It was so unusual for the lady's maid to say anything that her remark was greeted in surprised silence.

'Is she going?' asked Rainbird curiously.

'Yes,' said Felice. 'I am to alter an old gown of Miss Euphemia.'

'But she should wear white, surely,' said Jenny.

'White would not serve,' said the lady's maid. 'This colour will flatter her and I, myself, will arrange her hair.'

'I'm glad to hear it,' said Rainbird. 'Miss Jane has done nothing but mope about her room and ask morbid questions about Miss Clara.'

Felice's busy needle paused. 'Who is this Miss Clara?' she asked.

'The Honourable Miss Clara Vere-Baxton,' said Rainbird. 'The Vere-Baxtons were our second tenants after the death of the old duke. Miss Clara was very beautiful. A great tragedy.'

'Was?' Felice's black eyes looked intently at the butler.

'She was found dead in the Green Park near the reservoir without a mark on her,' said Rainbird.

'Miss Jane's been asking all sorts of questions like, 'What did she die of? She must have died of something.' I told Miss Jane that the physician, Mr Gillespie, could not find any explanation of her death.'

'I'm sure if anyone can give Miss Jane a bit of town bronze it will be yourself,' said Joseph, gazing with open admiration at the lady's maid. Lizzie felt a sharp pain somewhere in the region of her heart.

'In any case, it's unhealthy for little Miss Jane to be left alone to brood about such things,' said Rainbird, 'with only a servant like myself to talk to.'

They all clucked and shook their heads in sympathy. It was indeed a sad state of affairs when the gentry had to rely on such as themselves for conversation.

Upstairs, Jane was content that she was to attend the rout. She had longed to ask her mother whether a certain Lord Tregarthan would be present, but did not dare, knowing her mother's curiosity would be roused and also that Euphemia would tease her to death.

The idea of a party was lovely. Jane naively thought it would be a jolly affair with, perhaps, some dancing, never having met anyone who had been to a London rout. The social columns had been no help, for they only described who had been at various routs without pointing out the lack of refreshments or amusements.

Euphemia's gown was to come from Madame Duchasse, one of London's leading dressmakers. Jane knew her own gown was to made be out of one of Euphemia's old silks. She did not find this state of things unfair although she often chided herself over her own jealousy. It was surely natural that the elder and fairer should claim all the attention.

Jane adored the butler, Rainbird, since she saw a side of him that he hid from the rest of her family. She was vastly amused at the way the butler cleverly manipulated her mother into opening the purse strings a little wider. It had not taken the astute Rainbird long to find out that it was Mrs Hart who was head of the household and not the silent Captain Hart.

So Jane dreamt sensibly of meeting some pleasant gentleman who might find her interesting enough to chat to, and put Lord Tregarthan firmly to the back of her mind.

The rout was such a squeeze, such a crush, that it was doubtful if poor Jane, who had been placed in a corner of the back parlour and told to stay there, would have met Lord Tregarthan but for two factors.

Before the rout, the normally abstemious Rainbird had drunk long and deep, and Euphemia had been rude to him.

Rainbird, finding he had money in his pocket for the first time in many months, slipped out to The Running Footman, that pub frequented by upper servants, and there met Blenkinsop, Lord Charteris's butler from next door.

Blenkinsop was complaining about the load of coal he had found in the cellar. He had ordered the best quality before they had left for the country, he said, and now, by some strange miracle, the same quantity was there but it was of the cheapest imaginable.

Rainbird set out to divert Blenkinsop's mind from the coal by gossipping about his new employers and did not notice that he himself was drinking often and quickly as he talked. A quantity of gin-and-hot on an empty stomach – for Rainbird had not had time to eat that day – put him high in his altitudes, and, when he returned to Clarges Street, he felt like quite a different person: much grander, taller, and stronger and almost like the owner of the house instead of its butler. But, unfortunately for him, Euphemia was crossing the hall as he entered.

'Where have you been?' she snapped. 'Mama has been ringing and ringing and Jane has not had her tea taken up.'

'I will see to Miss Jane's tea immediately,' said Rainbird, forgetting his place and letting a flash of dislike for this small-minded beauty show in his expressive grey eyes.

'Miss Jane! Miss Jane!' jeered Euphemia with a toss of her curls. 'There is too much running about after my little sister. It is *I* who am making the come-out. This rout is in my honour. Jane is to sit in the back parlour and not draw attention to herself. I shall be watching *you* very carefully,' said Euphemia, looking the butler up and down. She turned on her heel and marched up the stairs. Rainbird watched her go. It was amazing, he reflected, how an ugly character destroyed even the greatest beauty.

Rainbird had received many slights, snubs, and put-downs in his career. What servant has not? But the excess of gin he had drunk had made him prickly and sensitive, and he was consumed by an unusual desire to get even with Miss Euphemia.

The first guests were nearly due to arrive when Mrs Hart sent word down to the kitchens that she meant to break with tradition and serve wine to the gentlemen and negus to the ladies. The normally stingy Mrs Hart was suffering from her first attack of 'stage fright' and was convinced that were her guests well-lubricated they might be more charitable. The servants ran hither and thither to wine merchants ordering last-minute deliveries.

Euphemia, dazzlingly beautiful in a pink sprigged silk gown and with a pink gauze turban atop her curls, sipped delicately at a glass of negus from the bowl that Rainbird had just prepared and set over a spirit lamp in the front parlour. Negus was a mixture of hot sweetened wine and water. She made a face and said, 'La! It tastes very watery. Do not continue to line your pocket at mama's expense, Rainbird. Take this away and strengthen it.'

'I will arrange it to your satisfaction,' said Rainbird, taking the huge silver bowl off the spirit lamp and heading for the door. Only Jane saw the wicked smile beginning to curl his mobile mouth.

'I'll negus 'er,' he muttered, setting the bowl on the kitchen table. He poured the contents off into a large jug and then proceeded to fill the bowl with sugar, wine, brandy, gin, and arrack. Satisfied at last, he held a glass out to the cook. 'Here, Angus,' he said. 'Tell me what you think of that.'

'Ladies' muck,' said the cook, tossing it off in one

gulp. Then he gasped and spluttered and clutched onto the kitchen table for support. 'I' feg,' he said hoarsely. 'I feel as if ah've been kicked in the bread basket.'

'Excellent,' said Rainbird primly. He straightened his waistcoat, picked up the bowl, and carried it upstairs, arriving in the parlour just as the first carriages were drawing up outside.

As well as the downstairs drawing room, which was formed of front and back parlours, Mr and Mrs Hart's bedroom upstairs and the dining room next door had been cleared of furniture for the rout.

All the world had heard that Mr Brummell was to be present and so society started to arrive in droves.

Jane sat in her corner, smoothing down the silk of her gown, and looking about her with wide eyes. She did not feel like herself at all. No one, not even Jane herself, had realized before that evening that she had a very pretty bosom. The rich burgundy silk of the gown, daringly cut by Felice's wickedly clever fingers, flattered her skin, making it look warm gold in the candlelight. Her thick hair had been brushed and pomaded until it shone, revealing little fiery lights in its blackish-brown tresses.

Euphemia had stood rather shyly beside her mother and father to receive the guests, but one glass of Rainbird's concoction had done wonders for her, and now, to Jane's surprise, for she had expected Euphemia to be more modest in her behaviour in London, her sister was laughing and flirting in a decidedly *fast* way.

In fact even Mrs Hart was laughing in a loud, rather vulgar manner. All the guests were sampling the negus. Rainbird's new brew was extremely popular.

There was a sudden silence and then a craning of heads as Mr Brummell made his entrance. The crowd surged into the front parlour and Jane was left to herself. The double doors that normally separated front and back parlours were open.

Jane supposed that many of the guests were famous. They certainly *looked* as if they expected to be recognized and admired. She fought down a feeling of disappointment as her wide eyes scrutinized the gentlemen. They were as studied in their manners and attitudes as the ladies. They had very loud drawling voices and wore dark evening dress with white silk stockings, cambric shirt fronts, and elaborate and intricate cravats and carried little flat chapeau-bras under their arms. As they talked, they filled out their conversation with many little bows, opening and shutting of snuff boxes, and flicking of lace handkerchiefs.

There was another little pause in the conversation, and then the babble of voices rose again. Another notable had obviously arrived. The newcomer was Beau Tregarthan with Mr Nevill at his heels.

'What a crush!' exclaimed the beau to Rainbird as he handed over his stick in the hall. 'And where among all these ladies am I to find the beautiful Miss Hart?' Euphemia and Mrs Hart were now mingling with their guests and Mr Hart was standing moodily by the window, looking out into the street.

Rainbird looked up into Lord Tregarthan's handsome face. Such a prize should not be handed over to the cruel and insolent Euphemia. 'Miss Hart is sitting quietly in the back parlour, my lord,' said Rainbird. 'If you will follow me . . . my lord . . . Mr Nevill, instead of announcing you, I can lead you from the hall through a door that leads directly to the back parlour.'

'Lead on,' said Lord Tregarthan cheerfully. The rout seemed to be an unusually noisy one. It was odd, all the same, that such a renowned beauty as Miss Hart should choose to sit quietly apart from the company.

Rainbird bowed before Jane and said, 'Lord Tregarthan and Mr Nevill are desirous of making your acquaintance, Miss Hart.'

Confronted by the man of her dreams, Jane jumped up like a jack-in-the-box, blushed painfully, and sank into a deep curtsy. 'I-I am n-not Miss Hart,' she stammered. 'I am Miss Hart's younger sister, Jane.'

Lord Tregarthan looked down at the diminutive figure, liking the clear candour of her eyes, the innocence of her face combined with the startling sophistication of her gown. 'Pray be seated, Miss Jane.' He drew up a chair beside her and turned to Mr Nevill. 'Peter, be so good as to find us a glass of whatever it is they are drinking.' Mr Nevill left and Lord Tregarthan turned his attention back to Jane.

'They are all very merry,' he said. 'It is unusual to serve anything to drink at a rout.'

'I did not know that,' said Jane. 'It is not at all what I expected. I thought there might be dancing and cards and things like that.'

'No, no,' he said seriously. 'A rout is a form of suffering. One comes to see and be seen, to be crushed, to have one's feet stepped on, but certainly not to enjoy oneself. Ah, thank you, Peter.' He took two glasses of negus from Mr Nevill, handed one to Jane, and kept the other one himself.

'Lord Dudley is over there, Peter,' he said, 'talking to himself as usual. It is a pity that no one ever listens to him.'

'Perhaps I will supply him with an audience,' said Mr Nevill, moving away and correctly interpreting that his friend, for some odd reason, wished to be alone with this strangely dull-looking younger sister.

Jane sipped her negus and choked. Lord Tregarthan tried his and then gently removed Jane's glass from her hand and put it on the edge of a marble stand that held a candelabra.

'Too strong for one of your tender years,' he said. 'It tastes more like a lethal form of punch than negus. It is supposed to be negus, is it not?'

'Yes,' said Jane. 'My sister told Mr Rainbird – that's our butler – to take it away and strengthen it.'

'He did – most effectively.'

He saw Jane's face fall in disappointment and looked up. Mrs Hart had come rushing up with Euphemia in tow. Lord Tregarthan rose to his feet and bowed. Mrs Hart introduced herself and Euphemia. Lord Tregarthan bowed again. His first impression of Euphemia was that of one of the most beautiful girls he had ever seen; his second, that she was slightly drunk; and his third, that she had a most unpleasant expression in her lovely eyes.

'You must not waste time with our little Jane,' said Mrs Hart. 'There are so many people desirous of making your acquaintance.'

Lord Tregarthan raised his quizzing glass and looked at Mrs Hart with one large magnified blue eye. Then he let it fall. 'I am tolerably content with my present company,' he said gently. 'You must not neglect your other guests.'

Mrs Hart flushed and turned away. Already many of the guests had surged to the upper rooms. There was a loud crash of glass from the dining room followed by a cheer. She hurried off. Euphemia stood her ground.

'It's your bedtime, Jane,' she said sharply.

'How could anyone sleep in all this hub-bub?' asked the beau. 'Please, I pray you, Miss Hart, do not trouble yourself over your sister. She will do very well with me.' He sat down again, swinging his chair round so he was facing Jane and with his well-tailored back to Euphemia. There was nothing left for Euphemia to do but to follow her mother, but her beautiful eyes flashed a warning to Jane of reprisals to come.

'Oh, I *do* wish, you know, that you had not elected to stay with me,' said Jane, much distressed.

'It does not become you, sir, to use such as I to humiliate my mother and sister.'

He raised thin brows. 'I did not humiliate them, although they seemed to me to want to humiliate *you.* Are you not considered marriageable?'

'No, my lord,' said Jane firmly. 'This is not my come-out.'

'Odd. One would have supposed your mama would have wished to save herself a deal of money by presenting you both at the same time.'

Jane looked at her hands. They were trembling slightly so she bunched them in her lap. 'I am not a beauty,' said Jane in a low voice, 'nor shall I ever be fashionable.'

He looked at her consideringly. 'Your eyes are fine and the warmth of your colouring is most unusual and attractive. In order to be fashionable, it is necessary to cultivate some sort of eccentricity. What would do for you? Perhaps you could walk backwards to Brighton? Smoke cheroots? Now, there is Lord Alvanley over there. *He* always has apricot tart on his sideboard, morning, noon, and night. The man with the sharp nose over there is Lord Petersham. He has the finest snuff cellar in Europe. It was also he who told his valet to put six bottles of sherry beside the bed and call him the day after tomorrow.'

'I notice they are all gentlemen of whom you speak,' said Jane, fascinated. 'What of the ladies?'

'Ah, there you have me!' he cried. 'Not one of the fair sex has ever really *tried* to cultivate eccentricity.'

Jane laughed. 'How can we discuss such frippery things? One would not think we were at war.'

There was a stillness behind the blue eyes and then they were merry again. 'What think you of my waistcoat?' he asked. 'I found this material in Rome. If you look closely, you will notice a fine stripe running through the silk.'

Jane battled with a feeling of disappointment. This dashing hero of her dreams was interested only in tailoring and gossip. In truth, Jane persuaded herself she was fighting with her disappointment when in fact she was secretly nurturing it. Deep down inside her a warning voice was telling her that this lord was far above her and that she might be on a threshold of love, a love more deep and mature than she might be able to bear.

'It *was* you,' she said in a low voice, 'that beat Jack Death?'

'That was quite some time ago. Yes, it was I.'

'I was there,' said Jane.

'At a prize fight?'

'I was only ten years of age. I dressed so that people might take me for a boy, but I fell out of a tree and the blacksmith recognized me and sent me home.'

'Just as well,' said the beau, much amused. 'Lots of blood.'

'Why did you fight?' asked Jane. Her hands were tightly clasped and her eyes beseeching. If only he would once more be the dream hero of her imaginings.

'Well, I had a great deal of money on my Fancy, to be sure, and when the fellow took sick, what else could I do but fight myself? What a terrible mess I made of my hands. I bathed them in Olympian Dew for weeks afterwards to try to restore them to their former whiteness.'

'Oh,' said Jane dully. So he had fought merely for money and his only subsequent worry had been the whiteness of his hands. But what else would he fight for? jeered a little voice in her brain. The love of a fair maiden? His king?

'Why is this house unlucky?' she realized he was asking.

'It is because the Duke of Pelham hanged himself here,' said Jane, 'and Miss Clara Vere-Baxton, daughter of the tenants a year after that, was found dead in the Green Park. I am very interested in Miss Clara, you know. You see, no one could find out how she died. There was no mark on her body.'

'Of course, it is up to us to find out how she died,' said Lord Tregarthan, taking a pinch of snuff.

'Us?' said Jane weakly.

'Why not?'

It was then Jane caught the jealous glances thrown in her direction by a group of ladies in the front parlour. Lord Tregarthan was a Catch. She might have persuaded herself that he had fallen from his pedestal, but it was wonderful to be envied for the first time in her life. Besides, he had liked her eyes and the colour of her skin. Jane sat up straighter and unfurled her fan. 'How shall we go about it?' she asked.

'I shall take you driving tomorrow and we shall discuss the matter. Dear me! How very noisy and rough this rout is becoming.' Lord Tregarthan cocked his handsome head as more sounds of loud cheering came from above followed by screams and bangs and thumps. He rose to his feet. 'Your servant, Miss Jane.'

Jane rose, curtsied, and then watched him leave. He stopped to chat to various people, his fair head and broad shoulders towering above the other guests. Then he was gone. He had not said what time he would call for her or whether he meant to ask Mrs Hart's permission. Jane hoped feverishly he would not forget. Fallen Idol he might be, but it would be so pleasant to watch the look on Euphemia's face as she, Jane, drove out with the most handsome man in London.

Lord Tregarthan had actually gone in search of Mrs Hart to request her permission to take Jane driving. He found that lady in her dining room on the upper floor in a high state of agitation. Several boozy bucks were trying to lower one of their number from the window to the street by his cravat because he had boasted he used so much material that, unwound, it would stretch from the window to the ground.

In their enthusiasm, in their crowding around the window, the members of the *ton*, lushy to a man with the effects of Rainbird's concoction, knocked over the tables and chairs, broke a pane of glass opening the window, and were now laying bets on the length of the cravat as the young man was lowered to the street outside amid cheers and yells. The betting fever rose and the two men holding onto the length of material, which once was an intricately tied cravat, forgot what they were doing while contesting the odds, and let go. There was a crash from the street outside and a scream of pain. After a short, startled silence the betting started up again as to whether he had broken one leg, two legs or his neck. Anyone going down to check, looking out the window, or going to help would be automatically disqualified.

Euphemia, jostled and forgotten in the wave of gambling fever shared by men and women alike, pouted and sulked. She pouted and sulked even more when the handsome Lord Tregarthan accosted her mother for the sole purpose of asking permission to take Jane driving. It was all Felice's fault, thought Euphemia, raging inwardly. She had turned Jane into a Cyprian with that low-cut gown.

Lord Tregarthan collected his friend Mr Nevill, and the two gentlemen made their way out past the young man of the cravat, who was painfully crawling back in on his hands and knees.

'How did you fare?' asked Tregarthan. 'Hope you didn't drink any of that negus.'

'Didn't have the time,' said Mr Nevill. 'I say, you will never guess who Mr Hart is!'

'No, who?'

'Why, he is none other than Captain James Hart of the *Adventure*.'

There was a certain stillness about Lord Tregarthan and the blue gaze he turned on his friend was suddenly sharp and inquisitive. 'You are sure?'

'Course I am. I recognized the man the minute I saw him. There he was, one of the heroes of England, jammed in a corner and looking like a funeral. To think that brave man with his little frigate of fourteen small guns and a crew of fifty-four men on board took that Spanish Frigate, *Infanta*, with her crew of three hundred.

'Nelson once said Captain Hart had more dash and Hair than any man in the service.'

'Why does our hero mope in London with a war to be fought?' asked Lord Tregarthan curiously.

'Women!' said Mr Nevill in tones of deepest contempt. '*He* did not say so and *I* did not ask, but it was all too evident that pushing, vulgar wife of his made him sell out. I shall call on them again, but only when I can be assured of meeting Captain Hart.'

'What of the beautiful Euphemia?'

'She should drink less,' said Mr Nevill roundly. 'She went from bold to brash to sulky to petulant, all in the space of half an hour.'

'Perhaps our beauty is not to be blamed. That so-called negus was evil stuff.'

'And what of you?' asked Mr Nevill. 'You caused no end of a buzz – the great Beau Tregarthan paying court to a plain schoolgirl.'

'Is she plain?' asked Lord Tregarthan, stifling a yawn. 'I confess I had not noticed. Let us talk of other things . . .'

FIVE

Poising evermore the eye-glass
In the light sarcastic eye,
Lest, by chance, some breezy nursemaid
Pass, without a tribute, by.

C.S. CALVERLEY, *HIC VIR, HIC EST*

It is a sad fact that no heroine is as sweet and virtuous in real life as she is in, say, a Grimms' Fairy Tale, and Jane, who had escaped early to bed and therefore evaded Euphemia's reprisals, awoke the next day with a mild, pleasurable, gloating feeling.

She would be swept off by Beau Tregarthan in his carriage while Euphemia, pale and wan, chastened and jealous, stood at the window to watch her go. Felice would become her devoted slave, cultivating the approval of the younger sister to counteract the mean temper of the elder.

And so it was with something closely approaching pique that Jane, descending late to the dining room, found Euphemia and the lady's maid on the best of terms. They had their heads together and were laughing over an illustration in a magazine when Jane entered.

The clever Felice had met all Euphemia's recriminations with amazed surprise. How could such a beauty suggest that a few stitches had transformed a little schoolgirl into a rival? The compliments and blandishments went on and on until Euphemia almost purred.

Then bouquets and poems had begun to arrive, all for Euphemia. The fact was that Mrs Hart's drunken rout had made her and her elder daughter social successes. A rout was not a fashionable rout unless it left you with something to talk about, and never before had there been such a rout as the Harts'! Two *tonnish* ladies of impeccable breeding, inebriated by Rainbird's 'negus', had tried to scratch each other's eyes out. The young man who had been dropped from the window had sprained both his ankles, although some thought he must have broken his neck, because from that day forth he went about in a cravat made of yards and yards of the strongest linen in case anyone should try to lower him from a great height and he indeed looked like the victim of a carriage accident.

Everyone had behaved so wonderfully disgracefully that Euphemia's bad manners were quite forgotten and only the image of her great beauty remained in the fevered brains of the gentlemen of the *ton* the following day as they struggled to quench their raging thirsts with bumpers of hock and seltzer.

Society wagged heads, gossiped, and laughed over the dreadful happenings at Mrs Hart's rout and declared her to be an Original. At one point during the evening, Mrs Hart, a trifle disguised, had broadcast to all and sundry the size of Euphemia's dowry. The necessary gilt-edge was added to Euphemia's beauty.

Now, dizzy with success, Mrs Hart appeared in the dining room, announcing that little Jane must have some new gowns, and disappointed Jane noticed that that pronouncement did not raise even one gleam of jealousy in her sister's eye. For it transpired that the great and powerful Marquess of Berry was to call to take Euphemia driving. What was a mere lord like Tregarthan compared to a marquess?

Besides, Mrs Hart, although pleased and surprised at what she termed 'Jane's little success', assumed that Tregarthan was merely amusing himself by entertaining such a young miss. Several ladies had been at great pains to point out to Mrs Hart that Tregarthan was a high stickler and that all his many mistresses had been divine beauties.

Euphemia, who had had this gossip of her mother, no longer considered Jane a rival and laughed and glowed while Jane sulkily helped herself to toast and tea and felt smaller and plainer by the minute. But her normally sunny disposition soon asserted itself and she slipped off to the kitchens to pump Rainbird about the late Miss Clara and so to have a fund of gossip to pour into the ears of Lord Tregarthan.

Jane had naively supposed that the servants would be delighted to have a visitor from upstairs, but the servants were irritated by her presence, and Mrs Middleton looked openly shocked that this young member of the gentry should not know her place – which was abovestairs.

Undaunted, Jane looked curiously at the members of the household staff she had not seen before – at the cook, MacGregor, at Lizzie, the scullery maid, and at Dave, the pot boy.

She averted her eyes from Lizzie, however, after that first look. There was something about the small scullery maid that reminded Jane painfully of herself. It was so much easier to imagine that one had undiscovered mysterious facets of attraction when one was not being faced with a near mirror-image. Like Jane's, Lizzie's hair was dark brown, and she had the same waif-like appearance and short figure. But where Jane's skin was golden-brown, Lizzie's was pale, and Lizzie's eyes were pansy-brown where Jane's were hazel.

'What can we do for you, Miss Jane?' asked Rainbird. He was feeling very tired. He and the others had been up most of the night, moving the furniture back into place and clearing up the mess. Although Mrs Hart did not get to bed until three in the morning – the bed that had to be carried back upstairs by Rainbird and Joseph – that sturdy matron had risen with the lark and had started to ring for attention and service instead of sleeping until two in the afternoon like any other respectable member of the *ton*.

'I wanted to find out a bit more about Miss Clara,' said Jane, feeling awkward under Mrs Middleton's openly disapproving eye.

'Come through to the servants' hall,' said Rainbird tolerantly. The dining-room bell began to jangle.

'Answer that, Joseph,' said Rainbird over his shoulder as he led Jane out of the kitchen.

'Meh feet,' moaned Joseph. He wore shoes two sizes two small for him because he considered small hands and feet aristocratic. Now his tortured toes looked like globe artichokes. He longed to escape to The Running Footman for a comfortable coze with Luke, the footman from next door. Never before had Joseph had such fascinating gossip to relate. Never before had he seen so many top members of the *ton* gathered under one roof and all of them behaving badly.

'Sit down, Miss Jane,' said Rainbird, pulling out a chair at the table in the servants' hall. Jane sat down, and Rainbird, after some hesitation, decided he was too weary to observe the conventions and sat down as well.

'The most marvellous thing has happened, Mr Rainbird,' said Jane, wide-eyed. 'Lord Tregarthan is to take me driving this very afternoon and he has agreed to help me find out what happened to Miss Clara.'

'It was not anything sinister or mysterious as I have already told you,' said Rainbird. 'If Mr Gillespie, her physician, could find nothing the matter, then her death must have been caused by some rare disease. These rare diseases come and go. In my youth there was a plague of something the doctors called Whirligigitis, but you never hear of that these days. Besides, the crowner passed a verdict of accidental death.'

Jane frowned. 'Did she have a beau?'

'Her parents wanted her to marry a Mr Bullfinch. Mr Bullfinch is extremely rich.'

'Did she love him?'

'I never considered the matter,' said Rainbird. 'Ladies do not often make marriages of affection. It was considered a fine match by her parents.'

'After her death, did Mr Bullfinch marry anyone else?'

'No. He was grief-stricken.'

'He could have been tortured by a guilty conscience?'

'Mr Bullfinch is a very respectable gentleman,' said Rainbird repressively. 'I have heard he is in London for the first time since Miss Clara's death. No doubt you will meet him.'

'Is he handsome?'

'Miss Jane,' said Rainbird with a sweet smile, 'you should not be belowstairs. You will get me in bad odour with Mrs Hart.'

'Meaning you want me to go away.' Jane stood up with a sigh. 'Wicked Mr Rainbird. *You* should be in bad odour with mama because you made all her guests tipsy.'

'*I?*' Rainbird opened his eyes to their fullest. He

took five oranges from a bowl on the table and started to juggle them. Jane laughed and clapped as Rainbird stood up, and, still juggling, led the way out.

Jane ran lightly up the stairs to her room. The very idea of going out in London was exciting, particularly as she had not seen very much of the city since her arrival.

Her bedroom overlooked the street, Euphemia preferring the larger, quieter room at the back. A noise from the street below drew her to the window. A group of acrobats was performing in the street outside. There were two men in soiled pink tights and a girl in a tawdry spangled dress. Jane watched them idly while her mind drifted back to that bright, brave image of Beau Tregarthan, which was fading fast to be replaced by the all too plain reality of a sleepy lazy lord with the dress of a Corinthian and the mind of a fop.

'You should not encourage that child, Mr Rainbird,' said Mrs Middleton after Jane had left.

'She's a taking little thing,' said Rainbird indifferently. 'I doubt very much if such a great man as Lord Tregarthan will encourage her in her funny ideas. Miss Jane told me that Lord Tregarthan had promised to help her find out who killed Miss Clara.'

'Then he should know better than to make fun of the girl,' said Mrs Middleton. 'Murdered indeed! If murder had been done, then Mr Gillespie would have discovered it. Who is Miss Jane to doubt the word of a gentleman who has attended no less a personage than King George himself?'

'I thought Miss Clara was ever so sweet and pretty,' said Alice dreamily. 'Lovely hair she had, masses and masses of it. A sort o' chestnut. Too good she was for the likes of Mr Bullfinch.'

'I never knew whether Miss Clara was as sweet and kind as she chose to appear,' said Rainbird. 'I always thought there was something sly about her.'

'Not her,' said chambermaid Jenny stoutly. 'Ever so kind to us, she was.'

Joseph swanned into the kitchen. 'There's talk again that the Prince of Wales might be made regent.'

'Such a thing!' exclaimed Mrs Middleton. 'Poor King George has come about before this. His madness is only temporary.'

'Some say,' said Joseph, who loved a gossip, 'thet the losing of the British colonies in America fair turned his brain.'

'And some think,' said Rainbird with a malicious twinkle in his eye, 'that we *lost* the colonies because of His Majesty's madness.'

'Sedition, Mr Rainbird,' cried Mrs Middleton in alarm. 'What if someone should hear you!' She looked anxiously up at the area window as if expecting to see a listening soldier.

Felice came into the kitchen to ask for hot water to make a pomade for Euphemia's hair.

Mrs Middleton bustled about. 'I'll put the kettle on,' she said. 'What else will you need?'

'A pennyworth of borax and half a pint of olive oil to go with a pint of water,' said Felice.

'Ah'll get it for ye,' said MacGregor eagerly.

'Sit down, Felice,' said Rainbird, drawing out a chair.

Felice sat down and opened the small workbasket she always carried with her and took out a half-finished piece of lace.

'Do you *make* lace?' asked Joseph, looking greedily at the delicate white froth in Felice's fingers.

'Yes. I was taught in France.'

'That would be before the Terror when you was a young woman,' said Jenny maliciously – meaning the French Revolution of 1789.

'No,' said Felice equably. 'I was only a child then.'

'Of course you were,' said Rainbird, giving Jenny a hard look.

'That lace would look lovely on a handkerchief,' said Joseph longingly.

Rainbird looked around for Lizzie and then remembered to his relief that she was out on an errand. He knew how much that present of Joseph's meant to the little scullery maid.

'Ta, ta, ta,' laughed Felice. 'Do not edge so close, Joseph. I will make a handkerchief for you.'

'*Thank* you,' said Joseph. 'When?'

'Joseph!' admonished Rainbird.

'Very soon,' said Felice with that small curved smile of hers. Joseph smiled at her dreamily. He could see himself producing that handkerchief in The Running Footman and flicking it under Luke, the next door footman's, envious nose.

'Mrs Hart is in high alt,' said Rainbird. 'Madam has seen fit to tell me that the Harts have been invited to a ball at Barcombe House in Berkeley Square next Thursday. If Dave will stay to guard the house, it means we can all take an evening off. I received many vails from our drunken guests last night. In fact, Lord Petersham was generous enough to give me something towards paying for the broken glass although I did not tell Mrs Hart *that.* So I suggest we stick to our old policy of dividing the money equally.'

'*Tiens!* How strange,' said Felice. 'Surely the upper servants should receive the largest amount.'

'Not in this house they don't,' snapped Jenny. 'We're one family, ain't we, Mr Rainbird? Or we were afore you come,' she added under her breath.

'What will you do with your free evening, Mr Rainbird?' asked Mrs Middleton, suddenly shy. Although Rainbird had never given her any encouragement, Mrs Middleton nourished a dream that the butler would one day propose to her when they both had a chance of retiring.

'As to that,' said Rainbird casually, 'I have a mind to go to the playhouse – if Miss Felice will do me the honour of accompanying me.'

Alice, the housemaid, looked slowly and wonderingly at the butler. The servants, in her innocent mind, had always been like brothers and sisters.

Rainbird was head of this kitchen family. The thought that the butler could have warm feelings towards a woman had not entered her mind.

Mrs Middleton looked ready to cry. Jenny muttered something and went out of the kitchen. Joseph, face flushed, was staring at the floor.

'Well?' asked Rainbird softly. His eyes were warm and caressing as they looked at the lady's maid.

Felice raised her black eyes from her sewing. 'Thank you, Mr Rainbird,' she said. 'I would like to see the play, I think.'

'John,' said Rainbird. 'My name is John.'

It was Jane who stood at the upstairs window to watch Euphemia leave, as the elder sister was to go driving first. At first Jane only had envious eyes for her sister's ensemble. Euphemia looked like a fashion plate. She was wearing an apron-fronted dress of white muslin, the skirt ties of which passed right round the body to form a bow under the bust. The neckline was edged with the frill of her chemisette. The gown had short, full sleeves, and a skirt with a short train and tucked hem. Over it, she wore a mantle with a frilled edge. Her little pointed shoes had ribbon ties and very low heels. Her hair was dressed *à la Titus*, that style which consisted of tousled curls confined by a bandeau, which went round the head and under the chin as well.

Then Jane turned her attention to the Marquess of Berry. He was a very tall thin man, quite old, perhaps about forty years. He appeared to have no chin at all, although his cravat was so huge and his shirt points so high it could have been buried somewhere among the folds of linen. He had great padded shoulders and a nipped-in waist. A bold black-and-gold-striped waistcoat, black coat, and thin shanks in black breeches gave him the appearance of a wasp. Euphemia seemed well content with her company.

At that moment Felice came hurrying into the room, exclaiming in horror when she found Jane still standing in her shift. She rushed out again to collect suitable items from Euphemia's wardrobe and at last she had Jane attired in a simple white muslin gown covered with a green silk pelisse that had very long sleeves with mancherons, frogging on the bodice, and a tucked hem. There was too little time to arrange Jane's hair properly, so it was twisted up on top of her head and covered with a pretty straw gypsy bonnet. Gloves, reticule, parasol, and fan were snatched up by Felice as she urged Jane downstairs.

When Jane entered the front parlour, it was to find Lord Tregarthan deep in conversation with her father. Mrs Hart was, for once, being ignored. Lord Tregarthan seemed reluctant to finish his conversation with Mr Hart, and, when he at last looked at Jane, his blue eyes were vague and dreamy and he did not appear to see her properly.

He made his bows and goodbyes and Jane was helped up into his carriage. It was a high crimson curricle with two bay mares harnessed tandem fashion in front of it. Lord Tregarthan in his fawn-coloured driving coat, leather breeches, and top boots looked every inch the Corinthian whip.

He had no servant on the backstrap. He waited until Jane was settled beside him and then he gently shook the reins, made a clicking noise, and the horses moved off, the sun shining on their silken flanks.

There was a great deal of traffic in Piccadilly, and his lordship muttered something about it having been better to go by Curzon Street. Then he raised his voice. 'I trust the Park will not be too dusty. Nothing but volunteers drilling and marching. I think we have more soldiers in London than we have fighting the French.'

Each district had its volunteers – the Bloomsbury Volunteers, the Chelsea Volunteers, the Clerkenwell Volunteers, and so on. The fear of Napoleon had been carried well into this new century. There were troops, volunteers, and pressed-men in such numbers that 1,500 were encamped in St George's Fields, 1,000 at Blackfriars, 1,000 at Tower Hill, 1,200 at the Foundling Hospital, and 2,700 in Hyde Park.

A pretty housemaid in a print cotton gown walked along Piccadilly past the carriage just as he had finished talking. Her dress was disgracefully short – it showed nearly the whole of her ankles. The beau cast her an appreciative glance.

Jane did not want him to look at pretty housemaids, or anyone other than herself for that matter. She bit her lip in vexation. Euphemia would be in

Hyde Park with her marquess. All at once Jane knew that Euphemia would make a point of accosting them with a view to claiming all of Lord Tregarthan's attention.

'I do not want to go to the Park, you know,' said Jane brightly. 'I have not been out and about before and I know nothing of London.'

A flash of amusement darted across his eyes as he looked at her. 'Then we shall go about London. Anywhere in particular?'

Jane dumbly shook her head, feeling very shy and young. He neatly wheeled the curricle about in the middle of Piccadilly, seemingly oblivious to the curses and shouts of the other drivers, and started threading his way down Piccadilly in the opposite direction.

'This is the centre of the *ton* universe,' he said turning down St James's Street. 'No lady must be seen here unescorted. That dirty big place with the clock at the end is St James's Palace.'

Jane hung tightly onto the guard rail and gazed about her in delight. She was to have London, and Beau Tregarthan, all to herself for one splendid hour.

They came out on Westminster Bridge after a stately progress down Whitehall and past the Houses of Parliament. The coffee-coloured River Thames rolled beneath with bluff-bowed barges drifting down its bosom.

'Whither away?' called a voice. A racing phaeton painted bright yellow had come along on their left-hand side.

'Good day, Cully,' called Lord Tregarthan. 'Showy pair of tits you've got there.'

'Best cattle on the market,' said a brutal-looking man with an insolent stare.

'Sir Cuthbert Armstrong – "Cully",' murmured Lord Tregarthan.

'Race you from Streatham Common to the Greyhound at Croydon,' called Cully.

'Really, Cully. I have a lady with me.'

'Thought it was your niece or something,' said Cully, raising his hat and glaring at Jane. 'Pity. I would lay you a monkey I could get there first.'

'Oh, please let us race him,' cried Jane, wriggling with excitement. 'I have never gone very fast before, you know.'

'Very well,' said Lord Tregarthan. 'Hey, Cully, the race begins at Streatham. You may follow us.'

'I'll see you there!' called Cully defiantly, and set off at a spanking pace.

'He'll wind his cattle before the race even starts,' said Lord Tregarthan. 'Miss Jane . . . may I call you Jane? You are so much younger than I.'

'Yes,' said Jane, feeling suddenly low. 'Are you very old?' she ventured after a short silence.

'I am thirty.'

'That is not old *at all*,' said Jane, although she privately thought it was. Somehow, she had believed that although the years had passed for her, Lord Tregarthan would stay ageless, frozen in time, waiting for her to grow up.

'Do you think Mrs Hart would appreciate my

taking her youngest chick on a race?' asked the beau.

'No,' said Jane. 'But then, I shan't tell her.'

'I feel I am behaving very badly,' said Lord Tregarthan. 'But I have accepted the bet. I will give you shillings for the turnpikes. Be ready to throw them so that I do not need to slow my pace.'

As they approached Streatham Common at last and saw Cully waiting in his phaeton, Jane felt so excited she thought she might be sick. She braced her feet against the splashboard in nervous anticipation. To her horror, she heard her companion say in his lazy drawl, 'I'll give you five minutes' start if you'll double the bet.'

'Done, you madman,' agreed Cully, grinning, and then he was off like the wind.

It seemed the longest five minutes Jane had ever known. The wind ruffled the new leaves of the trees on the Common and the birds sang. The sun beat down and a few people stopped to stare at them.

'We will discuss the interesting demise of Miss Clara when we get to Croydon,' said Lord Tregarthan. He took out his watch and looked at it thoughtfully.

Then Beau Tregarthan set his horses in motion and raised his whip.

Z . . z . . a . . ck! went the long thong, striking the air over the horses' ears.

'Oh, dear,' mumbled Jane as they surged forward.

SIX

In Tudor times the invitation to quarrel or combat was given by a biting of the thumb; in the middle of the eighteenth century, by cocking the hat; later by a jerk of the thumb over the left shoulder, implying illegitimate birth; in the early nineteenth century by the thumb to the nose, and within living memory by two fingers jerked upwards.

THOMAS BURKE, *THE STREETS OF LONDON*

People came shouting from the fields and houses as Jane and Lord Tregarthan shot past, believing their horses had run away with them. Faster and faster flew Lord Tregarthan's bay mares with their hooves rattling and their manes flying. The wheels hummed and buzzed while the curricle swayed, every joint and rivet creaking and groaning. Lord Tregarthan opened his mouth only to shout to Jane to throw a shilling to the toll keeper. Sometimes the press of traffic grew thick, but he threaded his way expertly through it. Once clear, he drove faster and faster until fields and houses were a flying blur.

All at once, at the top of a hill, appeared a flash

of yellow wheels through a cloud of dust. 'We have him!' cried Lord Tregarthan. He stood up and fanned his whip over the horses, the thong cracking over their heads without once touching them.

It seemed incredible to Jane that the horses could go any faster, but the gallant mares surged up the hill as if the sight of the quarry had lent them miraculous strength. Jane found herself yelling encouragement to them, praising them, promising them sacks of sugar loaves, *anything*, if only they would catch up with the dreadful Cully.

At last they were abreast of him, the rumps of the horses exactly in line. There was hardly an inch to spare in the breadth of the road and any moment Jane expected to be thrown with the jar from a locking wheel.

Then they were past.

Barely a moment too soon, thought Jane, feeling limp with relief and reaction as Lord Tregarthan slowed his team to a trot and drove up to the front of the Greyhound. The landlord came running out with gin and gingerbread, but Lord Tregarthan smiled and waved the offering away. 'We shall be stepping inside for some refreshment,' he said. 'Boy, go to their heads.'

An ostler ran up and seized the reins. There was a rattle of wheels on the road as Cully, with a face like thunder, drove straight past.

'Will he not pay you?' asked Jane.

'Yes. He will send a servant round with the money later. That is his way. A wickedly bad loser is Cully.'

Jane had to wait patiently until Lord Tregarthan saw his mares rubbed down and petted and fussed over. Then he led the way into the inn and soon they were both seated in the coffee room. They were the only customers. Feeling shy again, Jane sipped lemonade and wondered what her mother would say. One hour was the acceptable amount of time allotted to any gentleman taking a young lady out driving. Surely more than an hour had passed.

As if reading her thoughts, Lord Tregarthan said, 'I will tell Mrs Hart the pole broke if you wish, and then we may be comfortable. I am accounted quite a catch, you know,' he went on, his blue eyes mocking. 'She might see me as a future son-in-law. She will not be angry.'

'I fear mama thinks I am your latest whim rather than your latest love.'

'While we both know it is neither,' he said. 'We are both interested in finding out about Miss Clara.'

'Yes,' said Jane in a small voice, wishing his interest in her was that of a man for a woman. Not that she loved him, she told herself fiercely. It was only that it would be pleasant to be admired.

'What have you found out about Clara?' asked the beau.

Jane repeated the gossip she had had of Rainbird.

'I did not get any further,' he smiled, 'except that I learned that Mr Harry Bullfinch will be at the Quesnes' ball in Berkeley Square on Thursday. Do you attend?'

'I have been invited, but whether mama will take me is another matter,' said Jane.

'I shall speak to her about it on our return. What of Mr Gillespie?'

'I thought perhaps you might go to see him,' said Jane eagerly. 'I am not allowed out and could certainly not approach him on my own.'

'Has it always been thus?' he asked curiously. 'Are you always kept indoors?'

'Oh, no,' said Jane. 'In the country, you know, I was much freer, although nobody came to call except Lady Doyle. You know Lady Doyle, of course.'

'More a case of . . . of course not. Should I?'

'Lady Doyle says she knows everyone in the *ton*.'

'I have been out of the country. No doubt she escaped my notice. Where does she reside?'

'Upper Patchett.'

'Dear me. And is Upper Patchett the latest fashionable spa?'

'N-no. It is only a little village near Brighton.'

'But Lady Doyle spends a great deal of time in Town?'

'No,' said Jane, surprised. 'I have never known her to go to London.'

'In that case, how can she know so many of the *ton* if *she* does not go to London and *they* certainly do not go to Upper Patchett?'

'I often thought she told fibs,' said Jane. 'But you see how we are straying from the subject of Miss Clara, which is *much* more interesting. What is Mr Bullfinch like?'

'Very regular. About my age, I think. Well thought of.'

'How disappointing!'

'Were you looking for a sinister rake?'

'Something like that,' said Jane ruefully. 'Dear, dear. I begin to feel silly. I have been making mysteries where none exist.'

'On the other hand,' he pointed out cheerfully, 'everyone dies of *something*.'

Jane brightened. 'How very true and how very reassuring of you to say so.'

The beau tilted his chair back and crossed his booted legs. 'Now we will talk of things that really matter until I find out more about Mr Gillespie. Do you want to be a success at the ball?'

'Yes,' said Jane wistfully, 'but I fear I do not know how to go about it.'

'There is a new fashion in gowns – silk, not muslin – old gold with a green stripe. Not from Madame Duchasse but from an as-yet unknown Leonie of Conduit Street. And have your hair cropped.'

Jane blushed. 'You should not know about ladies' gowns,' she said severely. 'Besides, I cannot. I will probably have to have one of Euphemia's old gowns altered, although mama did promise me some new things.'

'That seems unfair.'

'Euphemia is so very beautiful and the elder,' pointed out Jane loyally. 'It is fitting all the best should be done for her.' She played nervously with the handle of her parasol while he raised his quizzing glass and studied her face.

At last he let it drop, and said mildly, 'You get the beauty of ladies like your sister all at once. But you – there is so much to discover.'

'What?' asked Jane eagerly, craving praise.

But his eyes were mocking as he swung his glass by its long golden chain. 'One day I will give you a list of all my discoveries,' he said.

A strange, companionable silence fell between the beau and Plain Jane. The wind moved the chintz curtains at the coffee room windows and sun and shade dappled the rough grass of the lawn outside.

At last he suggested they should take their leave. As he bent to pick up his hat and cane, he said in a more serious tone of voice than he normally used, 'Tell your father I shall call on him at eleven tomorrow morning. I have something important to ask him.'

'Yes,' said Jane breathlessly. Her eyes were like stars, but Lord Tregarthan, holding the door open for her, did not notice. A heady feeling of triumph made her feel faint. There could only be one reason why a gentleman told a young lady he wished to call on her father. Lord Tregarthan meant to ask permission to pay his addresses to her.

Jane floated out to the curricle.

Although they made the journey back at a sedate pace, the countryside and the houses swam past in the same blur before Jane's dazed and happy eyes. The whole of London would talk about her. Jane Hart. Jane Hart, who had snared the most handsome man in London!

They turned into Piccadilly from St James's Street and were about to turn off into Clarges Street when Jane clutched hold of the guard rail and cried, 'Stop!'

Surprised, Lord Tregarthan reined in his horses.

'Joseph!' screamed Jane. 'They are killing Joseph,' and before he could stop her, she had leapt nimbly down from the carriage and had started to run in the direction of the gates of the Green Park.

Joseph had been out on an errand. He had been sent by Mrs Hart to buy pink ribbons to trim a gown – a job that Joseph considered beneath his dignity. He mutinously decided to take a stroll in the Green Park, for the day was fine and he was reluctant to return to Number 67 and spend the rest of the day fetching and carrying.

He saw three ruffians bending over something and shied nervously away. Joseph was frightened of the lower orders, who often delighted in tormenting liveried footmen.

Then he heard a plaintive miaow. Some horrible fascination drove him forward to have a look. One of them held a cat pinned to the ground. It was one of the largest cats Joseph had ever seen, with a brown-and-gold-striped coat. It had golden eyes, beautiful eyes, which seemed to look straight to Joseph for help. Another ruffian took out his penknife. 'Let's poke the moggie's eyes out,' he said.

'Yus,' agreed his friends gleefully.

Somewhere right down inside Joseph's selfish, sensitive, cringing character, a voice said, 'No, you don't,' and, to his horror, he realized the voice had issued from his own lips, not in a mumble, but in loud, clear tones.

The ruffian who was holding the knife straightened up. 'Wot did you say?' he demanded.

Joseph opened his mouth to say, 'Nothing,' and to let his shaking legs carry him away, but his legs would not move and his voice said loudly, 'Leave the cet alone. Thet cet belongs o' me.'

The ruffians started mincing up and down, their hands on their hips, imitating Joseph's affected voice. They had let the cat go.

'Run,' pleaded Joseph silently to the cat. 'Run away and I will run with you.'

But the cat stayed, crouched against the ground. The leader of the ruffians, he who had held down the cat, turned and put his thumb to his nose and waggled his fingers at Joseph.

'Miaow,' went the cat.

Joseph had never accepted a challenge before. Never. The last time he had been in a fight had been with Luke, the Gharterises' footman. But Luke had not even asked him if he wanted to fight. He had simply set about him.

Again he waited for his brain to tell his legs and feet to move. Instead his brain told him to take off his black-and-gold coat and lay it carefully on the grass.

'A mill!' cried the leader's two companions. The

leader himself spat on his hands and approached Joseph. But the leader winked at his two companions and all three set on Joseph.

For the first few moments, sheer terror combined with mad rage served Joseph well and he sent two of them flying. Neither Rainbird nor MacGregor would have recognized the normally effeminate footman in the Joseph who landed punches with the finesse of Mendoza and the strength of Jackson. But two of them finally managed to seize his arms and swung him round to face the third, who drew back his fist ready to demolish Joseph's face.

Joseph closed his eyes.

Miraculously the grip on his arms slackened and there were cries of alarm and a female voice screaming, 'Help! Murder! Get the watch.'

Joseph opened his eyes. Jane Hart was jumping up and down and thumping Joseph's would-be assailant on the head with her parasol.

'The Quality. It's a gentry mort,' yelled the leader. They took to their heels down the park in the direction of Buckingham House. Past Jane, in full pursuit, thundered Lord Tregarthan. While Jane clutched Joseph, they both saw Lord Tregarthan catch up with the ruffians and Joseph screamed with glee as bodies started to fly.

'Lord Tregarthan will be hurt,' said Jane, making to run to him.

'Not he,' crowed Joseph. 'He's done wiff 'em already.'

They waited while Lord Tregarthan strolled back

towards them, ruefully examining a split in his driving glove. He did not seem either ruffled or out of breath.

'Splendid, my lord,' said Joseph. 'Oh, how splendid.' Then he sat down on the grass and began to cry. Lord Tregarthan looked on in a mixture of amusement and exasperation as Jane, oblivious of the gathering crowd, sank down onto one knee and peered anxiously into Joseph's tear-soaked face.

'Are you hurt, dear Joseph?' she pleaded. 'Do stop crying and tell me what I can do. Oh, here's a cat. Shooo!'

'No,' said Joseph. ''S my cat.'

He scrubbed his eyes with his shirt sleeve and leaned down and stroked the cat. It rubbed itself against his knee and purred.

'The *kitchen* cat, Joseph?' asked Jane.

'Yes, yes,' gabbled Joseph. 'Kitchen cat. Champion will rats, 'e is. Take 'im 'ome.' He rose to his feet, gathering the great brown-and-gold cat into his arms as he did so. It lay in his arms and regarded Jane with an insolent golden stare.

'Now, young fellow,' said Lord Tregarthan severely. 'An explanation, if you please. My curricle is blocking the traffic in Piccadilly right at this moment and Miss Jane is distressed.' He raised his quizzing glass and surveyed the circle of people about them. 'If the vulgarly curious would please leave, unless anyone likes a taste of my fists, I might be able to hear you.'

Nervously, the crowd began to edge away. Still

rattled by the occasional dry sob, Joseph told his tale, omitting, however, to say he had never seen the cat before.

'Highly commendable,' said Lord Tregarthan dryly. 'Take that animal away. And do not forget your coat.'

Jane handed Joseph his coat and, still clutching the cat, he went off, carrying his coat over one arm.

'What very odd servants you have, to be sure,' said the beau. 'Come, Miss Jane, and I will take you home.'

After he had returned Jane to her mother with smooth apologies for having kept her so late, he begged permission to call on Mr Hart in the morning and took his leave.

It was only as he was driving along Curzon Street that a sudden horrible thought struck Lord Tregarthan. At the same time, he heard himself being hailed from the pavement and saw his friend, Mr Nevill, who sprang lightly up beside him. 'Why so glum?' he asked.

'Tell me, Peter,' said Lord Tregarthan in a neutral sort of voice, 'if you told a young lady you intended to call on her papa on the morrow, what would she think?'

'Why – that you had marriage in mind.'

The beau drove on in silence.

'I say,' said Mr Nevill, 'never tell me you've asked leave to pay your addresses to the Hart chit!'

'No. I desired to see Captain Hart with a view to discussing a purely masculine matter.'

'Which is?'

'Entirely my affair. If anything comes of it, I will let you know. However, I fear I may have given both Jane and Mrs Hart the wrong impression.'

'Did you make love to the girl?'

'No, of course not. She is much too young.' He gave a rueful grin. 'But I tell you, Peter, there is something about that little waif that makes me behave in the oddest fashion. She did not want to go to the park, but requested a drive about London. Then, when we were on Westminster Bridge, the wretched Cully challenged me to a race from Streatham to Croydon, and before I knew what I was about, there I was, enjoying myself immensely, going like the devil, with Jane Hart cheering me on.'

'Did she?' Mr Nevill looked at his large friend in awe. 'A Trojan of a girl.'

'Not only that,' said the beau, 'she then involved me in a fight in the Green Park because her footman was under attack.'

'You know, you had better watch,' said Mr Nevill. 'I have never known you behave in such an unconventional manner. Are you sure there is not a certain something about Jane Hart which . . . ?'

'Do look,' interrupted Lord Tregarthan. 'Isn't that fellow a veritable quiz? His cravat is so high, he has to stare at the sky as he walks along.'

Mr Nevill began to laugh and the subject of Jane Hart's attractions was soon forgotten.

Although Lord Tregarthan was quite sure Jane

herself would not expect a proposal of marriage, her mother was another matter. He decided to send a note round that very evening to Mrs Hart explaining that the matter he wished to discuss with Mr Hart was one of business. He called his butler and handed him the note, his butler handed it to the first footman, who handed it to the second footman, Abraham, and Abraham set off in the direction of Clarges Street.

He was a young man who had but lately joined Lord Tregarthan's establishment. He was tall and good-looking but still naive and countrified and rather overpowered by the *tonnish* ways of the London servants.

He met Rainbird, who was standing on the steps of Number 67 taking the air. Perhaps if he had stated his business immediately the note would have been delivered, but, feeling at ease under Rainbird's benign look, he said he was from Lord Tregarthan's household and that he had but lately come to town. One thing led to another and soon Abraham was confiding his fears of grand society and Rainbird was giving him various tips as to how to go on.

Then there came the sounds of a noisy altercation from the kitchen below, and Rainbird invited the young footman down the area steps, saying he would settle the matter in a trice. The cause of all the row turned out to be Joseph's cat. MacGregor was threatening to behead it, Jenny and Alice were screaming it had a nasty look and, as sure as eggs were eggs, the animal had fleas, Joseph was clutching the cat to his bosom, Mrs Middleton was bleating in dismay, and Dave was joyfully taking one side and then the other. Lizzie was standing a little away from the argument, wondering what best she could do to aid Joseph.

The noisy freedom and interchange of views amazed Abraham, who was used to the stiff formality of Lord Tregarthan's servants' hall. He thought Alice was the most beautiful maidservant he had ever seen and if she did not want the cat then the cat should go. Abraham cheerfully joined in the argument.

Lizzie quietly fetched a saucer of milk and some scraps of beef. She gently took the cat away from Joseph and carried it to a corner of the kitchen, crouching protectively down beside it while it fed. Lizzie thought it was a strange-looking cat, more like a wild animal than a pet, but if Joseph loved it, then she would love it too.

Soon the bells began to ring. Mrs Hart, amazed and bewildered and overjoyed by Lord Tregarthan's request, had listened to Jane's tale of how the beau had suggested she patronise Leonie and had gone to see that person immediately, dragging Jane, Euphemia, and Felice along with her.

Now she was back, and, not finding Rainbird on hand to open the door or Joseph to carry in parcels, she was ringing the bells in the front and back parlours, striding from one room to the other, jerking the bell cords so hard that the bells up on the kitchen wall were fairly jumping on their wires. The cat was forgotten as the servants sprang to their posts.

Abraham cheerfully said goodbye and promised to call again. He walked back through the dusk, congratulating himself on having found new friends. London did not seem such a hostile and foreign place any longer. It was only when he reached his own servants' hall and was asked sharply whether he had delivered the note that he realized it was still in the pocket of his tails. Fear of losing his employ made him say, 'Yes.' He would find some way of slipping out later and delivering it.

But he was put to clean the silver, then he had to trim the lamps, then he had to carry coal, for the evening had turned chilly, then my lord arrived home for a late supper and he had to scramble into his best livery and powder his hair and take up his stance in the dining room.

After all that, the house was locked up for the night and all hope of taking the note round to Clarges Street had gone.

SEVEN

I have heard a traveller from the wilds of America say that he looked upon the Red Indian and the English gentleman as closely akin, citing the passion for sport, the aloofness and the suppression of the emotions in each.

SIR ARTHUR CONAN DOYLE, *RODNEY STONE*

Euphemia was every bit as jealous as Jane had ever wanted her to be, and Jane found herself not enjoying it one whit.

The elder sister made a point of visiting Jane in her bedchamber before she went to sleep to pour into her unwilling ears all the rakish exploits of Beau Tregarthan that Euphemia had managed to pick up from the Marquess of Berry. The marquess had failed to tell Euphemia that the beau had recently returned from the wars and so Jane was left with the picture of a Corinthian who pursued brutal sports as enthusiastically as he pursued every high flyer in Town.

'I pity you, Jane,' said Euphemia sweetly as she made for the door.

'No, you don't,' said Jane stoutly. 'You're jealous because *your* beau is old and looks like a wasp and *my* Lord Tregarthan is an Adonis.'

But the damage had been done. Jane lay awake, terrified. Were she to become engaged to Lord Tregarthan, then she would be expected to allow him to kiss and cuddle her. But what would that be like? Men had such brutal lusts – everyone knew *that*.

Her governess had once given her a talk on such matters, shortly before her services were no longer considered necessary. She had said that there were several things a lady must endure in order to present her husband with an heir. No lady enjoyed such things. One must close one's eyes tightly and think of one's country.

Euphemia seemed to accept this, but Jane had burst out in protest. What were all the love poems and romances about if it were all so unpleasant?

Love poems and romances were about *courtship*, the governess had said severely. That was the real and only honeymoon for a lady. The getting of babies was a different matter entirely.

So Jane tossed and turned, all her pleasure in being taken to a dashing dressmaker, all her joy in her new fashionable crop quite gone. She heartily wished Lord Tregarthan would cry off, forgetting he had not even proposed.

Then she heard a scream coming from away down in the bowels of the house. With nervous fingers, she lit her bed candle, and, shielding the flame, went to the door of her room and opened it.

The scream came again, louder this time.

A door crashed open in the attics and Rainbird came down the stairs, clad only in his nightshirt.

'It's Lizzie,' he said. 'The scullery maid. Go back to bed, Miss Jane.'

There was the sound of thumping from the attics as the other male servants got up.

Too awake and curious to go back to bed, Jane followed Rainbird down the stairs.

She entered the kitchen door at his heels.

Lizzie was standing on the kitchen table in her shift. Her eyes were wide and dilated. When she saw Rainbird, she pointed with a shaking finger to the floor.

Rainbird held his candle high.

In front of the hearth, neatly laid out, were three dead rats, five mice, and a large pile of dead black beetles. Standing beside them, its tail swishing backwards and forwards, was Joseph's cat.

Rainbird began to laugh.

'Come down, Lizzie,' he said, putting down his candle and lifting the shaking girl down from the table. 'The livestock is all dead.'

Joseph and MacGregor burst into the kitchen and stared in amazement at the kill made by Joseph's cat.

'Weel, that settles that,' said MacGregor. 'That animal stays.'

'I knew he'd be a good 'un,' crowed Joseph who had left his genteel accent behind him on his pillow. 'Think on't, Lizzie, they're better dead than running about all night.'

A gentle snore from under the table made them all laugh. Dave, the pot boy, was sleeping through all the commotion. The cat stalked forward and pushed MacGregor's leg with one paw.

'D'ye see that?' cried MacGregor. 'Was ever an animal so intelligent! Come along, Moocher, and I'll gie ye some gizzards.'

'Not Moocher,' wailed Joseph. 'I wanted somethink more h'elegant.'

'Now, Miss Jane,' said Rainbird severely, 'back to bed. The excitement is over.' He looked at her narrowly. 'You look troubled, miss. Is anything the matter?'

'No,' said Jane bleakly. 'Nothing at all.'

After they had all left, Lizzie settled down on her bed, which was a straw mattress on the scullery floor. She cringed as she felt the cat pressing against her. But Lizzie had long been afraid of the rats and beetles that came out when the other servants had gone to bed. It was the noise the hunting cat had made that had frightened her, not to mention the pile of dead creatures she had found on the hearth. She now realized if she encouraged the Moocher to sleep with her, she would no longer have anything to fear. And it was Joseph's cat.

'Puss, puss,' she murmured sleepily. The large cat butted her in the side with its head, then it curled up and lay against her, warm and comforting. Lizzie felt in her bosom for Joseph's handkerchief and smiled to herself as she fell asleep.

* * *

When Jane awoke the next morning all her fears had gone. What a fool she had been to listen to Euphemia! She rushed to the looking glass and admired her new crop of pomaded curls. She was only eighteen and had not even been out and yet she was to receive a proposal of marriage.

Although the ballgown had been ordered for the ball on Thursday, there had been no time to buy Jane a new gown for the proposal. Felice had worked over one of Euphemia's new ones and was soon on hand to help Jane into it.

Jane was to stay in her room until Lord Tregarthan had seen her father. Then she would be summoned to the drawing room and left alone with her beau. She had risen very early and was waiting at the window a full hour before Lord Tregarthan's curricle drew up outside the house.

To her surprise, although he had a liveried tiger in attendance, he was in carriage, rather than morning, dress: blue coat with brass buttons and leather breeches with top boots.

She waited and waited. The little clock on the mantel ticked away busily. Jane wondered what her father was saying. How terrible not to even know *what* one's own father would say. He could not turn down the offer – mama would not let him. But still . . .

What did her father ever think about behind that wooden expression of his? And for that matter, what did Lord Tregarthan think? What sort of man was he?

Tick, tick, tick went the busy seconds. Jane shivered in white muslin. The day was cold and blustery but a fire had not yet been lit in her room.

And then she heard voices below in the street and opened the window and leaned out.

Beau Tregarthan and her father had emerged from the house together. They seemed on the best of terms. In fact, Jane had never heard her father sound so animated. His voice floated up to her. '. . . miss it all,' he said, 'standing in the cockpit in an inferno of noise and powder smoke and yelling men with the rumble of the huge guns leaping at their ropes as they recoil, and the gunners shouting, "Steady! Stand steady!" as the crews run the worm down the reeking barrels to remove smouldering tinder, and then, "Run her out! Steady! Stand steady! Give fire!" and, oh, my goodness, the batteries going off like an awful clap of thunder . . .'

His voice dropped as he walked around the far side of Lord Tregarthan's curricle to examine it. He patted the horses. Captain Hart looked much younger than Jane could ever remember him looking. To her surprise, the beau and Captain Hart got into the curricle and drove off.

Jane closed the window and sat down, feeling bewildered. Surely any man who had just asked for someone's hand in marriage would want to see that someone immediately. A frown of worry creased her brow and she cocked her head. The house seemed very silent.

Gathering up her courage, she made her way

downstairs. Faint voices came from the back parlour. She found her mother and Euphemia inside. They both looked up as she entered. Mrs Hart's look was hard and disapproving. But Euphemia! The thing that made Jane's heart sink was the look of genuine pity in Euphemia's beautiful eyes.

'He did not propose,' whispered Jane.

'Of course not,' snapped Mrs Hart. 'What a man of Tregarthan's character and reputation is doing by misleading us so is beyond me. *You* should have known better, Jane. Now, look at the money I have wasted on an expensive ballgown for you, not to mention the horrendous expense of paying for it to be ready by next Thursday. At least, *both* my daughters are not disasters. Berry is coming to take Euphemia driving again.'

Jane tried to say defiantly that she did not care, that she would not have married Lord Tregarthan anyway, but a lump the size of a cricket ball seemed stuck in her throat.

'Mr Hart has gone to Fladong's in Oxford Street with Lord Tregarthan,' said Mrs Hart with a disapproving sniff. Fladong's was the hotel frequented by naval officers in the way that Slaughter's Hotel was for the army and Ibbetson's for the Church of England.

'He wished to go before, but I put my foot down. Of what use hankering over navy battles when those days are finished. But I could not very well say anything in front of Tregarthan.'

Jane left and went up to her room, hoping that when she was on her own, she would manage to accept with dignity that she had made a mistake, that Tregarthan had not meant a proposal. But Felice was waiting for her, Felice who, in that mysterious way of servants, already knew that my lord had not proposed.

'Sit down, Miss Jane,' she said, 'and we shall discuss milord.'

Jane turned her head away. 'What is there to discuss?' she said airily. 'He has gone out with papa, and that is no great matter.'

'You were given to understand he would propose to you this morning,' said Felice, 'and that *is* a very great matter.'

'I was mistaken,' said Jane stiffly. 'I should have used my wits. He does not care for me.'

'*Tien!* That is the talk of a child and not a woman. Attend me! Now, this Lord Tregarthan has taken you out driving, no?'

Jane nodded her head.

'He has never before given any young girl that honour. I heard him advise Mrs Hart to take you to Leonie's and he also added that he looked forward to seeing you at the ball. A man whose affections are engaged does things like that. You expect too much too soon.'

Jane shrugged. 'He thinks I am a schoolgirl.'

'Then stop behaving like one,' said Felice. 'You cannot expect any gentleman to propose to a girl without a dowry after such a brief acquaintanceship. Only heiresses are proposed to very quickly and the proposals always come from unsuitable fortune hunters.'

Jane smiled. 'You are very kind, Felice. I do not think I have heard you say so much before.'

'Well, now that I have begun to talk, listen,' said Felice. 'Now, madame does not wish my presence at the moment, so we shall begin your lessons.

'You must learn how to flirt, how to gossip, how to charm. I study these things, me, because I, too, may find a husband here.'

'But servants cannot marry,' said Jane, wide-eyed.

'I did not say anything about marrying a servant,' said Felice. 'There was no one I wished to marry in Brighton and Mrs Swann did not entertain, which is why I paid that Lady Doyle to recommend me for this post.'

'*Paid?*'

'Is it not done? Lady Doyle told me it was quite the thing. I had not had a post before Mrs Swann, you see.'

'Dear me,' said Jane. 'I fear, Felice, that Lady Doyle lies and lies to get money any way she can. We must tell mama.'

'No, do not do that. She might dismiss me. We shall expose Lady Doyle later. Now, to your lessons . . .'

The days before the ball flew by in a rush. No one had time to ask Mr Hart why he had gone off with

Lord Tregarthan. Euphemia and Mrs Hart were kept busy attending routs and assemblies. Euphemia's vouchers for Almack's had not arrived, but both she and her mother expected them any day. Jane was left at home. Mrs Hart felt she was already doing more than enough by taking her to the ball in Berkeley Square.

Downstairs, the servants were planning what to do with their evening off. All privately disapproved of Rainbird taking Felice to the play, particularly Alice, Jenny, and Mrs Middleton. He had never asked any of *them* to go to the playhouse. Besides, Felice was *French*, so Rainbird was not only being disloyal to his friends but downright unpatriotic.

Joseph had thought up several grandiose schemes but had finally rejected them all. Even the most practical one – that of meeting Luke, the Charterises' footman, for a drink – had fallen through as Luke was to be on duty that evening.

Alice, Jenny, and Mrs Middleton finally banded together and arranged to go to Vauxhall to see the fireworks and, for the first time, Joseph noticed the wistful look in Lizzie's eyes. He could not take her anywhere himself, he thought. Once, when they had all been staying in the country, he had found Lizzie very good company, but it had not mattered then, being away from London, that he should be seen talking to a mere scullery maid.

'What will you do, Lizzie?' asked Rainbird.

'I don't know,' said Lizzie sadly. 'Perhaps I shall stay here with the Moocher.' She leaned down and patted the gold-and-brown cat, which gave a growling purr and rubbed itself against her legs. Then it leapt lightly onto Joseph's lap and stared up into his face.

Joseph wriggled uneasily. He felt the Moocher was asking him to take Lizzie out. He felt Lizzie was asking him to take her out, as she looked at him with those large, pansy-brown eyes. To get away from both his adorers, he put the cat on the floor and, mumbling something about needing a breath of fresh air, made his way up the narrow stone-area steps.

Luke was returning back to Number 65, a flat package under his arm. 'Don't know what's up with them all this Season,' he grumbled when he saw Joseph. 'Run here . . . run there. Will's sick, so I got all the work.' Will was the second footman.

'And there's something else,' said Luke, slouching against the railings. 'I won the draw at The Running Footman. Fourth prize.'

'What d'you get?' asked Joseph. 'I didn't get nothing.'

'Two tickets for Astley's Amphitheatre.'

'So who're you taking?'

'Nobody. It's on Thursday and I'm on duty.'

'I'll buy 'em, half price,' said Joseph.

'Garn. Tell you what – three quarters.'

'You didn't pay for 'em,' said Joseph hotly.

The two footmen seemed set to haggle all night, but Blenkinsop, the butler, emerged from Number 65 and sharply called Luke to heel.

'All right, half price it is,' Luke said, shoving the tickets into Joseph's hand.

Astley's Amphitheatre at Lambeth was a wonderful circus, full of displays of horseback riding, acrobats, lurid plays, and spectacles. Joseph went downstairs fingering the tickets. Felice had entered the kitchen and was studying a recipe for a wash for the hair.

'What was all that argy-bargying about upstairs?' asked Rainbird.

'I was buying two tickets to Astley's from Luke,' said Joseph. 'He won them at the draw at The Running Footman. I got 'em half price. It's not as if he paid for them.'

'Who are you taking, Joseph?' asked Alice, patting her golden curls. 'I should love to go.'

'So should I,' chimed in Jenny.

'But you was going to Vauxhall,' complained Joseph.

'But Astley's is another thing,' said dark-haired Jenny. 'Come on, Joseph. Take one o' us.'

Joseph sat down. The cat sprang on his knee and he absent-mindedly stroked its fur.

'I'll take Lizzie if she'll go,' he said gruffly.

'Lizzie will go,' said Felice in the silence that greeted Joseph's announcement. Lizzie was clearly beyond speech.

'Well, that's settled then,' said Joseph, turning red under all the curious, staring eyes.

'My boy,' said Rainbird, standing up, 'come with me. I have a bottle of port I've just decanted and I would appreciate your judgment.'

Never before had Rainbird asked Joseph's opinion on anything. Joseph gave the cat a last affectionate pat and stood up. It was pleasant to be deferred to by Rainbird of all people.

'I must have growed up somehow,' thought Joseph in awe as he followed Rainbird into the butler's small pantry. 'Must be the cat. Like a father, I got responsibilities now.'

Euphemia's courtship by the Marquess of Berry continued at a sedate pace. Jane envied her sister. She did not envy her the marquess but rather her level-headed and practical approach to marriage. Euphemia was sensibly prepared to settle for a title and fortune without bothering her pretty head about love and romance. Jane had tried to get her to talk about the marquess, hoping perhaps to find out that Euphemia was secretly dismayed and frightened, but Euphemia was so complacent, it was ridiculous to assume she was plagued by even one doubt.

Jane had thought long and hard about Lord Tregarthan. It was still hard to make the switch from the dream lover to the real and present man. The dream Lord Tregarthan now appeared strangely boyish. In her dreams, he had rescued her from all sorts of perils and each dream had ended with him taking her in his arms and depositing a chaste kiss on her mouth.

In every fantasy, the elation she felt was always caused by the look on the watching Euphemia's face rather than by any passion engendered by the feel of his lips.

It was hard to picture Lord Tregarthan in reality as the giver of chaste kisses. He was too large, too virile, and too masculine for that. As the eve of the ball rushed upon her, Jane became tormented by new physical feelings she did not understand – an odd mixture of yearning and desire.

Under Felice's tuition, she had learned to sit gracefully, how to hold her fan – by the end, *never* by the handle unless when it was unfurled – how to sit down on a chair without looking round, how to parry a 'warm' flirtation, and how to behave in a sweet and demure manner if addressed by one of the formidable patronesses of Almack's.

The ballgown looked disappointingly simple to Jane, who nourished dreams of spangled gauze, which was what Euphemia would be wearing. Felice, however, crowed with delight when she finally slipped the dress over Jane's head. She led Jane to the long glass. Jane thought she looked rather odd. Admittedly, the gown, with green-and-gold stripes, was very dashing and showed her bosom to advantage. Her tousled curls had the frizz pomaded out of them and they glinted with reddish lights in the candlelight. Felice had found a pair of long, jade earrings from somewhere and long gold kid gloves. 'No ornament in your hair. You are so mondaine, you will be taken for a Frenchwoman.'

Jane looked at her doubtfully and then realized Felice was paying her a high compliment. But despite Felice's warm and welcome praise, Jane could not help wishing that she, Jane, looked more like an ordinary debutante – someone with light brown hair and a pastel or white gown – someone, in fact, like Euphemia. All in that moment, Jane realized how much she wanted to look like Euphemia, how much she had always wanted to look like Euphemia.

The Harts had rented a carriage for the evening. Mrs Hart knew that they could well have walked – Berkeley Square was only just around the corner – but it was unfashionable to arrive on foot, so they all had to set out one hour early to move the small distance, waiting and fidgeting behind a long line of other carriages.

What would Lord Tregarthan think of her gown? wondered Jane. It was so hard to tell what he thought about *anything*, or if he thought much about anything *at all*. It was considered vulgar and unmanly to betray any feelings whatsoever. Although that did not apply to Lord Tregarthan, who did not affect the studied and wooden expression of most gentlemen of the *ton*, the gentle, mocking humour in his eyes was, in its way, as much a barrier to his real feelings as the current fashionable fish-eyed stare. How pleasant it would be if she could make just one pair of masculine eyes light up at the sight of her.

Mr Bullfinch would be there. Better to concentrate on the mystery of Clara, instead of longing for masculine adoration, which always seemed to be for Euphemia and never for Jane.

When they were finally arrived, Jane's heart began to beat quick and fast. Even Mrs Hart and Euphemia fidgeted nervously as they mounted the steps to the ballroom. Only Mr Hart, wooden-faced as ever, stood patiently, seemingly unmoved and unimpressed by the grandeur around him.

Then Mr Hart turned and looked down at Jane. 'I think, Jane,' he said in a low voice, 'you will create a sensation. You have become a most *tonnish* young lady.'

Tears of gratitude filled Jane's eyes; she fumbled for her father's hard, calloused hand and gave it a squeeze.

Perhaps her father actually loved her, thought Jane in wonder. She had come to believe that maternal and paternal love were only to be found among the lower orders.

And then it was her turn to make her curtsy to their hosts, Lord and Lady Quesne.

She had an impression of a stout, cross-looking woman and a choleric man, and then she was in the ballroom. Quizzing glasses were raised in their direction, hard eyes glared and raked Jane from the top of her curls to the bottom of her gown.

There were hundreds of candles lighting the ballroom. Jane had never seen such a *glare* of candles.

She felt small and naked.

She wanted to go home.

She wanted to go back to Upper Patchett.

And then she saw Lord Tregarthan.

EIGHT

A public horse-whipping is an extremely disagreeable thing, and yet cases have been known when such have been administered by irate brothers or fathers, when the only fault committed by the young man had been to obey the commands of a forward and bold young woman – one of the sort to whom Hamlet would have said, 'Get thee to a nunnery.'

MRS HUMPHREY, *MANNERS FOR MEN*

Jane looked at Lord Tregarthan and could not look away. He was like a rock in this desert of coloured, shifting society sand.

He looked very grand in an exquisitely tailored coat of dark blue wool. He wore a ruffled shirt above a white satin waistcoat, breeches of buff kerseymere and white silk stockings. His flat black shoes had real diamond buckles instead of the paste ones being worn by many of the other men at the ball.

Jane knew she was attracting attention by standing staring at him, but she wanted him to come to her side so that she might not feel so alone in this alien world.

A group of men and women came up to him. Soon more guests arrived and all Jane could see of him was the back of his golden head above the moving, jostling throng.

Jane had never been out anywhere in the evening that was so brightly lit as this. At her mother's rout, there had been plenty of candles and lamps, but there had still been soft shadows in the corners. This was rather like being on stage.

She sat down next to Euphemia and looked at her fan. Euphemia was striking an Attitude and Jane thought it was very silly, so it was to cover her embarrassment as well as her fear that she kept her eyes down. Onc glimpse at her sister had been enough to show her that Euphemia had her hands clasped as if in prayer and her eyes were rolled up to the ceiling. Jane recognized the pose as Early Christian Martyr.

Several gentlemen came up to be introduced to Euphemia. Jane was aware of their presence, rather than seeing them, as her eyes were still on her fan, so she missed thc fact that many masculine eyes were also on herself. Thcn she heard herself addressed and, looking up, saw that Lady Quesne was ushering forward a thin, pimply gentleman who did not seem to know what to do with his hands or feet.

She introduced him to Jane as a Mr Jellibee, adding that Mr Jellibee was just panting to dance, and then left them together.

Mr Jellibee led Jane on to the floor. It was a

country dance, and Mr Jellibee had an odd way of leaping forward right onto Jane's feet.

Jane did her best and was thankful when the set finally came to an end. Mr Jellibee asked her if she would like some refreshment. Jane, anxious to be rid of him, refused. She was turning away to rejoin her mother, who was sitting with the chaperones, when she saw Lord Tregarthan standing with an imposing-looking woman.

Jane forgot all Felice's training. A quick glance behind her was enough to show her that Euphemia was happily engaged with the Marquess of Berry.

Jane marched up to Lord Tregarthan and said in a loud, strained voice, 'I wish to speak to you, my lord.'

He broke off his conversation and gazed down at her in mild surprise. The lady with him looked furious.

Lord Tregarthan turned to his companion. 'My lady, may I present Miss Jane Hart. Miss Hart, the Countess Lieven.'

Jane turned a fiery red and sank into a deep curtsy, wishing at that very moment she could sink through the ground. The countess was glaring at her.

Countess Lieven was a patroness of Almack's and the most formidable female leader of the *ton.* She often said, 'It is not fashionable where I am not.'

'As I was saying,' said the countess, pointedly turning a shoulder on Jane, 'we must strive harder to keep mushrooms out of the opera house.'

Lord Tregarthan gave Jane a sympathetic smile, but she turned and scurried away, her face flaming.

'And talking of mushrooms,' went on the Countess Lieven, 'we shall not be sending vouchers to the Hart family. I was in two minds about it, but if that sort of pushing behaviour is an example of that family, then we are better off without them.'

'Miss Jane is very young,' said the beau, 'and she knows I wanted to discuss a certain matter with her. Besides, it is not her come-out, you know, but the sister's.'

'And which is the sister?'

'Miss Euphemia Hart. Over there. Just taking the floor with Berry.'

Euphemia was laughing very loudly and flirting quite dreadfully.

'Do you know,' said the countess, 'I do believe she's worse than the younger one. Besides, the mother is most odd, as I recall. Tried to embrace Lady Jersey, claiming to have a mutual friend of whom no one has ever heard.'

'You must do as you see fit,' sighed the beau. 'Perhaps the Harts will survive without an entrée to Almack's.'

'No one,' said the Countess Lieven, 'survives without an introduction to Almack's. No one.'

Mrs Hart was busily engaged in talking to the lady next to her when Jane sat down on the other side.

Jane studied the toes of her silk shoes. She had behaved dreadfully, and she knew it. She could only be thankful her mother had not witnessed her behaviour. For any young lady to accost a man boldly in the ballroom, no matter how well she knew him, was beyond the pale.

She could feel herself burning up with mortification.

Then she saw a pair of smart black dancing pumps standing in front of her. Her eyes slowly travelled up a vista of silk stockings, knee breeches, waistcoat, and cravat to a dark, handsome face smiling down at her.

The gentleman half turned to her mother and said, 'I have been searching for Lady Quesne to beg an introduction, but she is nowhere to be found. My name is Eprey, James Eprey. May I beg a dance with this beautiful lady?'

Mrs Hart looked from him to Jane in surprise. Then she looked round cautiously as if expecting to see someone else.

'Certainly,' she said at last. 'My daughter, Jane.'

Jane stood up, curtsied, and gathered up her courage.

Now all Felice's instructions came back to her, and she danced gracefully through a Scottish reel with her new escort and promenaded with him at the end of the dance, listening to him with flattering attention. He said he had lately come to Town and was enjoying himself very much. He talked of the plays he had seen and the assemblies and routs he had attended.

When the next dance was announced, Jane

curtsied to him again and made to return to her seat. But she was all at once surrounded by a small court of gentlemen begging for the next dance.

It was not as if Jane had suddenly turned into a dazzling beauty. It was that her gown was stylish and attractive, her manners pretty and modest – the gentlemen had obviously not noticed her social gaffe with the Countess Lieven – and she looked pleasant and lively.

When Jane found later on in the evening that Lord Tregarthan had managed to secure a dance with her, she had by then regained her composure. 'Do you mind if we do not dance?' she asked. 'I am so very thirsty and, besides, I owe you an apology.'

'Ah, yes,' he said, leading her towards the supper room. 'I know why you wish to apologize, and yet you did not do anything so terribly wrong. It is just that young females are not expected to command the attention of gentlemen, unless they are hardened flirts of great fortunes, or demi-reps.'

'Euphemia will not now receive vouchers to Almack's,' said Jane miserably.

'I don't think she was going to get them anyway,' said Lord Tregarthan, seating her at a small table. 'That,' he said, sitting down opposite and waving his quizzing glass in the direction of the right-hand corner of the room, 'is Mr Bullfinch.'

Jane looked eagerly across the room. 'The gentleman wearing the green silk coat,' said Lord Tregarthan.

Jane saw a thick, heavy-set, ape-like man talking

to a pretty debutante. He wore his hair powdered, which made his blue jowls look darker. His eyes were brown and clever, just like a monkey.

Jane gave a dramatic shiver. 'He looks sinister. Only see how he is laughing and talking to that lady. Obviously he did not grieve much over the death of Clara.'

'I believe he was shattered by her death,' said Lord Tregarthan. 'I shall introduce you in a little. Now, let me tell you about my visit to Mr Gillespie, that eminent doctor.'

'And I suppose he was steadfast, upright, and charming as well,' said Jane pertly. 'You seem determined to refuse to supply me with a villain.'

'I regret to say he was polite and charming. I went as a patient, as I could hardly stroll in and ask him if he had murdered Clara.'

'What did you say was the matter with you?' asked Jane curiously.

'I was invalided home from Portugal with a bullet in my leg,' said Lord Tregarthan. 'I told him I still felt it stiff and asked his advice.'

'I did not know you were in Portugal. Why were you there?'

'Fighting for my country.'

'Oh,' said Jane in a small voice. 'I did not know.'

He studied her face curiously, and then smiled. 'You seem to know little of military matters. Perhaps you have little interest. Having a father who is such a great hero must make us all very small beer by comparison.'

'Papa? A hero?'

'Very much so. He fought bravely in the Battle of the Nile. And you must know he was at Trafalgar with Nelson.'

'I am afraid I did not,' said Jane. 'He never talks about anything, you see.'

'Well, to return to Mr Gillespie, he examined my leg and pronounced it a sound member, recommended more walking, and then charged me an exorbitant fee.'

'What is he like?'

Lord Tregarthan fell silent, remembering his visit. The doctor had been polite, polished, and efficient. He was, Lord Tregarthan judged, only a few years older than himself. He was of medium height with small, neat features, a triangular mouth fixed in a permanent smile, and small, grey, angry, humourless eyes.

'I cannot describe him properly,' said Lord Tregarthan at last. 'He reminded me somehow of a waiter with sore feet.'

'I do not understand.'

'He has risen from very humble beginnings to the top of his profession very quickly. He has cultivated a charming, deferential manner, but I sense contempt and anger inside. I wonder what he really thinks of all of us useless members of society.'

'A member of society who fights for his country is not useless!'

'How warlike you are! You forget there are many Whigs in London who consider the war a great waste of money on England's part and would gladly see Napoleon bring all his so-called liberty, equality, and fraternity over here.'

'How can anyone think that. The man is a monster!'

'Not quite the monster of the cartoonists and lampoonists. He does not eat children, whatever they may say. But he has great power and is very ruthless.'

'But to return to Mr Gillespie – you did not mention Clara?'

'No, but he is to call on me next week. I fear it was rather an odd move on my part to call on him. He is not used to members of society putting themselves out in such a way.'

'Mr Bullfinch is returning to the ballroom,' said Jane.

'And must pass us.' Lord Tregarthan rose to his feet. 'Evening, Bullfinch.' He performed the introductions. Mr Bullfinch introduced his lady companion. He turned to Jane and asked her politely whether she was enjoying the Season.

'Very much,' said Jane. 'We have rented a house that is most conveniently situated – 67 Clarges Street.'

Mr Bullfinch went very still. There was an air of listening about him, whether to hear if there was any underlying meaning in Jane's words, or to a voice from the past, Jane could not say.

'You are indeed fortunate,' he said, after a short silence. 'I, myself, live in Streatham, which is *very* inconvenient. I am looking for accommodation nearer the City, where I conduct my business. I hear the music beginning. Good evening.'

He led his companion away.

'Is Mr Bullfinch in *trade*?' asked Jane.

'In a manner of speaking. He is a banker. He is well-connected and well-liked. Society is not all sham and vanity. Mr Bullfinch is that rarest of all creatures – he is quite without pretension or conceit.'

'But did you see how still he went when I mentioned the house in Clarges Street?'

'Understandably. The love of his life who stayed there died in odd circumstances. Did you expect him to scream or break down and confess to murder or something like that?'

Jane burst out laughing. 'Yes, I did. You have the right of it.' Her laugh was gurgling and infectious. He found himself thinking how charming and refreshing she was. He found himself noticing the swell of her bosom and the roundness of her arms. Then he realized Jane was reddening under his steady gaze.

'We are to perform the waltz,' he said. '*Very* daring. Almack's has decreed that never, never shall such a vulgar display appear in their rooms. Do you waltz?'

'Euphemia and I used to practise it,' said Jane, remembering a rare happy day when she and Euphemia were friends.

'You may practise with me.'

Jane looked shyly up at him under her lashes. She could no longer remember the Lord Tregarthan of her dreams. He was real and alive and she wished he would take her in his arms and tell her he loved her. A startled look came across her face at this new realization.

'What are you thinking about?' he asked.

'I was wondering why you called on my father.' Jane took her courage in both hands. 'I fear you gave mama the wrong idea.'

'Clumsy of me. But not you?'

'No,' lied Jane. 'Of course not.'

'Mrs Hart had every reason to misunderstand the purpose of my visit. I thought later that I should explain myself better and sent her a note.'

'She did not go on as if she had received it.'

'So I put you in the suds again,' he said. 'Poor Jane.'

'Plain Jane,' she whispered miserably. 'That is what Euphemia calls me.'

'Dear me. How very jealous she must be of you. You are not plain. You look very fashionable and, to me, quite enchanting.'

Jane felt a heady surge of pleasure and delight. Lord Tregarthan cursed himself. One did not give a young lady of good family such extravagant praise unless the affections were seriously engaged, and he was sure his were not. There was something so touchingly lovable about Jane, which always acted on his senses and gave him a desire to make her laugh, to see her happy.

'Our dance, I think,' he said, rising and offering her his arm.

'It is too bad of Tregarthan,' fretted Mrs Hart. 'Just look at him! Jane is gazing up at him, head over heels in love. A man of his experience should have enough sense to depress such folly.'

'Oh, people always *like* Jane,' shrugged Euphemia, who had paused to fan herself between dances. 'I can never understand why. Certainly, it is always very low people in the village – always telling me what a darling child she is and stuff like that.

'Yes, people *like* Jane, but they don't fall in love with her.'

'Here is Berry come to claim his second dance,' said Mrs Hart complacently.

Euphemia pinned a glad smile on her face and hoped she would not stumble in the steps of the waltz. She must not. It would be too humiliating when Jane seemed to float through them, her feet barely touching the ground.

Lord Tregarthan delivered Jane back to her mother after the waltz was finished and then returned to join his friend, Mr Nevill, in the refreshment room. That gentleman was happily broaching his second bottle of port, declaring he had done his duty by dancing with as many wallflowers as possible.

'Not including Miss Jane Hart, however,' he said. Lord Tregarthan turned and looked back into the ballroom. Jane was already dancing with a new partner.

'She is a great success,' said the beau. 'It is a new thing for society to have someone so open and friendly and likeable in their midst. She is like a kitten, all play and friendliness and curiosity.'

'Aha, gone are our bachelor days.'

'I am not contemplating marriage. Are you?'

'Oh, no, not I,' said Mr Nevill with a knowing look. 'But watch out. I've seen it happen before to the most hardened bachelors. Besides, I thought it was your intention to find a wife this Season.'

Lord Tregarthan stretched and yawned. 'I've changed my mind, for one thing,' he said sleepily. 'And I'll tell you another. This is the first time in my life I have found the London Season such a bore.'

'Despite Jane Hart?'

'Despite Jane Hart.'

Jane danced on, hoping against hope that Lord Tregarthan would approach her again. There was so much she wanted to ask him. He had not even told her why he had wished to speak to her father.

Rainbird and Felice enjoyed the play immensely. They had gone to Covent Garden to see Mrs Jordan in *The Country Girl.* Although the performance had not found favour with the critics, Mrs Jordan could still sway her audience and so there was little rowdiness, apart from an incident when one young Pink of the *ton* climbed down from his box and walked across the stage on his hands and had to be pelted with oranges before he could be driven off.

It was enough for Rainbird to be with Felice. She

fascinated him. He wondered what went on behind that Mona Lisa smile of hers.

They repaired to a chop house after the performance and ate mutton pies and drank porter. It was only when they were walking home through the streets that Rainbird realized with a queer little pang that, although he had talked for a long time about himself and his life, he had learned very little about Felice. She was wearing a subtle perfume and the silk of her gown rustled as she moved. He longed to steal a kiss, and that longing increased the nearer he got to Clarges Street. He hoped the others would still be out so that they might have further opportunity to be alone together.

They were approaching the house when they saw Mr Hart arrive home alone. It was his keen sailor's eye that perceived them for, despite the new reflectors that had been put in the parish lamps, the street was still very dark. He nodded to Rainbird and then said, 'Felice – a word with you, if you please. Follow me.'

Felice looked momentarily startled, but she followed Mr Hart obediently through the front door. Rainbird walked closely at their heels, hoping Mr Hart would call for wine so that he might have an opportunity to find out why the usually withdrawn and silent captain wished to speak in private to his wife's lady's maid. But Mr Hart ushered Felice into the front parlour and shut the door in Rainbird's face.

Rainbird went sadly down the back stairs. But

before he had reached the servants' hall, the whole magic of the evening in Felice's company was on him again.

Lizzie was sitting alone in the servants' hall at the table, a dreamy look in her eyes.

Rainbird thought she was looking very fine. She was wearing one of the print cotton gowns that had been bought for her the year before, when they were in funds. Now it seemed to have an almost stylish air, and her soft brown hair had been elaborately dressed.

'You look like a lady,' grinned Rainbird.

'That was Felice,' said Lizzie. 'I was always scared of her, her being a Frenchie and all. But she come to me right after the ladies had left.

'She had taken my gown away earlier to "do something to it", she said. She had made it fit ever so well, and she insisted on doing my hair. Ever so kind, she was.' Lizzie blushed. 'Even Joseph said he wouldn't have recognized me.'

'Where is Joseph?'

'Gone to bed, Mr Rainbird. But we had such a wonderful time. Oh, the horses and the spectacles. I never saw anything like it before in my life.' She looked up with glowing eyes and saw her own expression mirrored in the butler's eyes. 'Are you in love, too, Mr Rainbird?' she asked.

'No,' said Rainbird sharply, gripped with fear for Lizzie, fear for himself. 'We cannot be in love, Lizzie. Servants must not fall in love. We cannot marry unless we are very lucky or very old.'

'Mr Rainbird!' piped a voice from the doorway.

Rainbird swung around. Dave, the pot boy, stood clutching a small bundle of letters.

'Why aren't you in the kitchen?' demanded the butler. 'Where have you been?'

'It was the Moocher,' said Dave. 'Well, it wasn't 'im, ezzactly. I wanted to see what the 'ouse looked like upstairs. So I was wandering abaht, not touchin' anythink, like. Well, arter all, I was s'pposed to be seein' everythink was all right. Anyways, the Moocher followed me up and when we got to the bedroom, 'e leapt into Miss Jane's room and jumped on 'er desk and 'is paws slipped an' 'e went thump, right into them little drawers. One of 'em sprang out like it was a secret drawer or somethink, an' these letters shot out.'

'You silly boy!' raged Rainbird. 'Why did you not leave them where they were?'

'I 'eard the capting comin' and I got frit.'

'Give them to me,' sighed Rainbird. 'They are probably just letters Miss Jane has been receiving from someone.' He took the package of letters and turned it over. It was tied with ribbon and wrapped around with one sheet of blank paper that concealed the name of the addressee.

Rainbird went wearily up the stairs. He paused in the hall, listening to the buzz of voices in the front parlour, and assumed the captain was still talking to Felice. He hesitated, longing to listen at the door, but finally he shrugged and went on up to Jane's bedroom. He strolled in without first scratching at the door, and then stopped in dismay. Jane was sitting at her dressing table, brushing her hair.

'I am very sorry, Miss Jane,' said Rainbird. 'I did not hear you return and the bells did not ring, so I assumed . . .'

'Mama is with papa,' said Jane. Her mother was so busy questioning him in the front parlour as to what he was doing talking to Felice, thought Jane, that she had not had time to disturb the servants. 'What have you there?' she asked.

'These letters were found by Dave, the pot boy. The cat escaped and he pursued it into your room. It jumped on the desk and a drawer sprang out. Dave should have replaced the letters. I am sorry.'

Jane stood up and went to the desk and examined the little drawer. Thoughts raced one after the other through her head. It was a secret drawer. What if the letters gave a clue to Clara's death? Rainbird would not let her read them if he learned they did not belong to her. If they had been sent by Mr Bullfinch, then Rainbird would – correctly offer to return them to that gentleman.

'Thank you, Mr Rainbird,' said Jane with her back to him, praying he had not examined the letters himself. 'I would be grateful if you did not mention finding them to my mother.'

'I promise,' said Rainbird, placing the letters on the top of the desk. 'But a word of caution, Miss Jane. I hope you are not encouraging some unsuitable young man to write to you. I do not recall any letters for you coming either through the post or being delivered by hand.'

Jane forced a laugh. 'These were sent to me while

I was in the country,' she said. 'Simply a girlish friendship. Her letters are vastly amusing. I hid them, for Euphemia takes delight in prying into my affairs.'

'Good night, then, Miss Jane,' said Rainbird.

'Good night,' said Jane.

She waited breathlessly until his footsteps could be heard descending the stairs. Then she lit more candles and sat down and untied the ribbon binding the letters.

She hesitated. It seemed awful to read someone else's correspondence. But perhaps the letters were very old and the person who had sent them was now dead. It would do no harm to make sure. Besides, how could she return the letters, supposing the writer were still alive, if she did not find out who had written them?

She opened the first letter and began to read. Colour flamed up into her face. The words seemed to scorch the very paper. She did not need to look at the signature to realize they were from Mr Bullfinch.

'My darling Clara,' he began, before plunging into such a cry of passion that Jane went hot and cold by turns. Even to her innocent mind, it became clear that Mr Bullfinch had known Clara more intimately than any gentleman had a right to know a lady before marriage. With shaking fingers, she opened the others and read them as well.

There was no doubt about it. Mr Bullfinch had been *obsessed* with Clara and had feared desperately that she no longer loved him.

Jane wondered what to do. It would embarrass Mr Bullfinch quite dreadfully if she returned the letters. But would not he perhaps betray some sign of guilt? Only look at what he had written in one of them – 'If you are not to be mine, I will make sure that no other man has you.'

Somehow, Jane decided, she must see Lord Tregarthan as soon as possible and ask his advice.

A frown creased her brow. She wondered why her father had wished to speak to Felice alone. What an odd business! Jane was suddenly too sleepy to wonder any more about the letters or her father's behaviour.

She fell asleep to the sounds of a waltz tune drifting through her head.

NINE

He wanted to be happy, he expected it, or he would not have married her.

Under all this selfish shunting of the responsibility of home happiness on to the woman's shoulders, lies a deep justifying truth – it is her business – and the fact that some of nature's laws, such as gravitation, are at times extremely irritating, does not, however, make them inoperative.

ANNA A. ROGERS

All at once, life became very flat and dull for Jane Hart.

Lord Tregarthan did not call to pay his compliments the day after the ball, but sent his servant instead with his card. That servant was Abraham, who found time to scuttle down to the kitchen to confess to Rainbird his failure to deliver that earlier note.

Rainbird pointed out that Abraham was unlikely to be found out now and to let the matter rest. Abraham stayed to flirt with Alice, greatly cheered by her response to his overtures. Alice thought him a very nice young man, but that was all. She encouraged his sallies out of a vague feeling of pique towards Rainbird. She had not forgiven the butler for taking Felice to the play. If he was interested in taking out any female, then Alice felt it should have been one of them – even Lizzie.

Mrs Hart became too involved in buying new gowns for Euphemia and basking in Euphemia's success with the Marquess of Berry to take Jane anywhere. Mrs Hart also failed to notice that her husband was furious with her.

She had berated him in her attempts to find out why he had chosen to see Felice in private. But, despite her taunts, accusations, and insults, Captain Hart had refused to say one word in explanation. By the time Felice herself had offered the quiet reason that Mr Hart simply wanted to know the meaning of some French phrases, Mrs Hart had forgotten about the whole affair, and also that she had called her husband a useless nincompoop, loudly regretting the day she had ever married him.

Only Rainbird noticed the blaze of anger in the captain's eyes when they rested on his wife. Jane was too absorbed in fretting over her housebound existence, and worrying about when she would see Lord Tregarthan again, to remark on it, and Euphemia was too self-absorbed.

As Mrs Hart's vanity over her daughter's success grew, so did her pettish temper. She now considered herself a leader of the *ton.* Things were bad enough, but one morning, a week after the ball, Mrs

Hart received a letter from the patronesses of Almack's refusing Euphemia vouchers.

Mrs Hart and Euphemia screamed and sobbed and would not be comforted. Only the recollection that the Marquess of Berry was to be their guest at dinner that night made them pull themselves together.

Mrs Hart had also asked Lord Tregarthan. She was sure he had no interest in Jane whatsoever, but London society had proved jealous and curious enough to show it believed there to be a gratifying *tendre*. Although Euphemia and her mother knew he was to attend, neither had thought to inform Jane.

Dinner was to consist of roast sirloin of beef, boiled shin of beef, boiled leg of mutton with caper sauce, a couple of rabbits and onion sauce, salt fish boiled with parsnips and egg sauce, puddings, jellies, fruit and nuts. MacGregor had also been asked to produce several side dishes 'in the French manner', Mrs Hart hoping to nonplus the cook, whom she did not like. But MacGregor had once worked in Paris and was delighted to have an opportunity to demonstrate his skill.

Felice helped Jane into the glory of the finest gown she, Jane, had ever worn. It had been delivered from Leonie – ordered for Jane when Mrs Hart had thought Lord Tregarthan was going to propose. It consisted of a pink gossamer satin slip with a Grecian overdress of white gauze fastened at the front with silver filigree. The bottom was trimmed with five inches of Vandyke lace. It had Spanish slashed sleeves confined with silver filigree buttons and cord. Her hair was dressed *à la Grecque* and ornamented with Persian roses. Shoes of white satin spotted with pink foil, long pink French kid gloves, and a white crepe fan completed the ensemble.

To her surprise, her mother entered and presented her with a pearl necklace and bracelet. 'We have a beau for you tonight,' said Mrs Hart, 'so I wish you to look your best.'

Jane's heart began to hammer. 'Who is he?' she asked tremulously.

'A Mr Bullfinch, my dear. A banker. Very wealthy.'

'Mr *Bullfinch!*' Jane stared at her mother in horror. What an incredible coincidence! 'But he is the man who was engaged to poor Clara.'

'And who is this poor Clara?'

'Why, Clara Vere-Baxton, the lady who was found dead in Green Park.'

'Oh, I heard something about that, but it was *centuries* before. Mr Bullfinch is a good catch.'

'So good that *I* may end up in the Green Park as well!'

'Jane! Either you behave prettily or you may keep to your room.'

Jane sighed. It would be lovely to stay in her room but, on the other hand, it was a wonderful opportunity to find out more about Mr Bullfinch. 'I am sorry, mama,' she said meekly. 'I shall behave.'

'See that you do!' said Mrs Hart grimly. 'And make sure Felice returns those pearls to me. You are only to have them for this evening. I hope this dinner is a success. I feel I have been too lenient with the servants here. Rainbird is all very well, but Joseph is dithery and lazy, MacGregor is a savage, and Mrs Middleton a fool.'

'Mama,' ventured Jane. 'I understand you had little hope of securing a husband for me, so why have you suddenly decided to produce Mr Bullfinch?'

Mrs Hart looked at her younger daughter and frowned. Gossip had it that Mr Bullfinch was unattached, very rich, very plain, and practically of the merchant class. For all those reasons, she thought he would do very well for Jane.

Mrs Hart, overwhelmed with social success despite her snub from Almack's, had begun to regard herself as a member of the aristocracy. She felt sure Mr Bullfinch would be well aware of the honour done to him and would be only too eager to find an excuse to ally himself with such an illustrious family.

She said, 'I always have your best interests at heart. Mr Bullfinch approached me at the Quesnes' ball. He was most gracious, and Lady Quesne urged me to further my acquaintance with him. If the Quesnes favour him, then he must be good *ton*.'

She patted Jane's cheek and left.

Jane took out Mr Bullfinch's letters. Perhaps if

she memorized one phrase and dropped it into the conversation, she could watch his reaction.

There was one line Mr Bullfinch had obviously written from some place in the country: 'The ice is now frozen on the ponds and lakes, hard and glittering in the sunlight, hard and glittering like your beautiful eyes when you look upon this, your devoted slave.'

It seemed rather hard to think about working that into a general conversation. Jane was about to search for another when the door opened and Felice stood there, waiting to take her down.

Jane was not prepared for her own reaction on seeing Lord Tregarthan again. He was standing in front of the fireplace, talking to Mr Bullfinch, as she entered. Candlelight glinted on his burnished hair and his blue eyes turned in her direction with a mocking, caressing look. Jane flushed to the roots of her hair and stood stock still. Felice had to give her a gentle push in her back to nudge her forward.

Jane made her curtsy to Lord Tregarthan. There was a roaring in her ears. She realized Mr Bullfinch was asking her whether she had enjoyed the Quesnes' ball. With a great effort, she pulled herself together and answered that she had.

'I have not seen you about,' said Lord Tregarthan. 'I sat through Mrs Gulley's musicale and I went to Summerses' rout, but never a sign of you, although I did see your sister.'

'I have not been out at all,' said Jane, gratified that he had missed her.

Mr Bullfinch smiled at Jane. Jane blinked up at him in surprise. He had a delightful smile, a warm smile, which lit up his face and gave him great charm. 'Perhaps I may persuade you to come driving with me, Miss Jane,' he said.

'Thank you, Mr Bullfinch,' said Jane.

'But not tomorrow,' said Lord Tregarthan. 'To-morrow is mine, is it not, Jane? Do remember you promised to allow me to take you out.'

He smiled down at her in that new caressing way of his, and Jane felt her knees turn to jelly. 'Yes,' she whispered, dropping her fan, and then bumped her head against his as they both stooped to pick it up.

'Your roses have slipped,' he said, gently touching her hair and straightening a battered blossom. 'There! Now you look like the gypsy princess again.'

Mr Bullfinch looked curiously from one to the other, bowed and walked away, and was soon engaged in conversation with Euphemia. The Marquess of Berry had not yet arrived.

'What is Tregarthan about?' hissed Mrs Hart behind her fan to her husband. 'He cannot want her himself so why does he not leave her alone? I only invited him to annoy that cat Mrs Wentworth, who is trying to secure him for one of her pasty daughters.'

'Mayhap he wants to marry her,' said Mr Hart curtly.

'Nonsense. He is merely amusing himself.'

'I do not think he is such a fool,' said Mr Hart.

'He would have a warm, loving wife in Jane, which, believe me, is far better than being married to a discontented fashion plate.' This last was said with considerable venom, but Mrs Hart had noticed the arrival of the Marquess of Berry and had fluttered off in his direction.

'You had not said anything about taking me driving,' said Jane shyly to Lord Tregarthan.

'Ah, but I meant to. I should have realized you would be kept prisoner. Do you not wish to go driving with me?'

'I should like it above all things. You see, I have something important I must tell you . . .'

'Dinner is served,' said Rainbird from the doorway.

The company, which consisted of six guests and the Harts, moved into the dining room.

Lord Tregarthan was seated opposite Jane with Euphemia on one side and an elderly lady on the other.

Jane had Mr Bullfinch on her right and a Mr Woodforde on her left.

Chambermaid Jenny had been exalted to the dining room in order to help Alice and Joseph. Beautiful odours rose from the side dishes placed before them. MacGregor had excelled himself.

Now although Mrs Hart's faith in Lady Doyle was waning fast, old habits and loyalties died hard, and Lady Doyle had told her that all the *ton* complained about their servants and it was accounted a fascinating topic of conversation.

Mrs Hart was taste deaf as some people are tone deaf. She picked gingerly at a dish of plaice covered in a delicious sauce *à la Matelote*. She all at once assumed that MacGregor would not know how to make French sauces, so she gave a shiver of disgust and looked behind her for Rainbird, who had gone to fetch a cordial for one of the elderly guests. She called Joseph.

'Take these side dishes back to the kitchen.' Then, raising her voice, added, 'My cook is a Scotch savage and has no idea how to cook French dishes. But you will find his plain cooking very good. Of course, our own staff in the country, which is *very large*, is very well trained.'

Lord Tregarthan raised his eyebrows and waved Joseph away as the footman tried to remove two of the side dishes at my lord's elbow. 'I must have a debased palate,' he said, 'for I swear your chef cooks like an angel.'

Mrs Hart hesitated. But it seemed such a grand, *tonnish* thing to do, to complain about one's cook, that she gave a brittle laugh and said, 'Well, we shall leave those beside you, Lord Tregarthan. Joseph, take the rest away immediately.'

Joseph piled up the dishes and carried them out.

Mr Bullfinch was talking to Jane about the horrible winter they had all endured. 'Ice everywhere,' he said with a shiver. 'I became tired of having to crack the ice in my water cans before I could wash in the morning.'

Jane saw her opportunity. 'That reminds me of

something I read,' she said. '"The ice is now frozen on the ponds and lakes, hard and glittering in the sunlight, hard and glittering like your beautiful eyes when you look upon this, your devoted slave."'

And then she shrank back before the blaze of anger in Mr Bullfinch's face. Lord Tregarthan tensed in his chair, watching them curiously.

'Miss Jane,' said Mr Bullfinch in a low, urgent undertone. 'You have obviously found some letters I wrote to Miss Vere-Baxton. How *dare* you read my personal letters? How dare you!'

'I am sorry,' whispered Jane, all at once appalled at the enormity of what she had done.

'Was it not enough,' went on Mr Bullfinch in that dreadful undertone, 'to lose the only woman I ever loved without having some *child* read my letters and then mock me?'

Tears welled up in Jane's eyes. Lord Tregarthan was about to break with convention and address a remark to her across the table when the door of the dining room opened with a crash and MacGregor stood bristling on the threshold.

Had Rainbird returned with the dishes, he would have known how to placate the fiery artist of the kitchen.

But Joseph, whose feet were hurting him, had merely thumped down the tray and said, 'Mrs Hart don't like your cooking.'

MacGregor had begun to tremble with rage. He tore off his apron and skull cap and headed for the stairs.

Now, still shaking, he glared at the assembled guests and finally focussed on Mrs Hart at the end of the table.

Rainbird appeared behind him, alerted by Joseph, who had rushed to tell him that MacGregor was on the warpath. 'Now, Angus . . .' he began, but the cook was beyond reason.

'Whit was the matter wi' thae dishes?' he demanded.

Mrs Hart glared back. Like many of the English of the period, Mrs Hart hated the Scotch with a passion. Bigotry and bad temper raged in her bosom.

'Leave the room this minute,' she said. 'Your cooking was returned because it was disgusting.'

'I am an artist,' howled MacGregor. 'An artist, do ye hear . . . you great, pudding-faced harridan?'

Captain Hart's wooden face cracked into a rare smile.

'*You*,' said the cook with loathing, 'are the commonest old frump I have ever wasted ma art on. Upstart *mush-room*. The hell wi' ye.'

'Take him down to the kitchens and bind him. He shall be horsewhipped,' shouted Mrs Hart.

Euphemia burst into tears and cried to the Marquess of Berry for protection.

Lord Tregarthan rose easily from his seat. He signalled to Mr Bullfinch and both men took the quivering cook gently by an arm apiece and hustled him out and down the stairs.

MacGregor sank into a chair at the kitchen table and burst into tears.

'Do we tie him up?' asked Mr Bullfinch, looking at the sobbing cook as Joseph and Rainbird came into the kitchen.

'No,' said Lord Tregarthan. 'I cannot understand Mrs Hart. My own chef is a volatile gentleman and I treat him with kid gloves. This man cooks like an angel. Listen, MacGregor, I shall find a place for you.'

The cook dried his eyes and looked miserably round the kitchen. He saw Rainbird and held out his large red hand like a child holding out its hand to its father. Rainbird took the cook's hand and sat down at the table beside him.

'Better take my lord's offer and leave now before you're whipped,' said the butler.

'I cannae leave ma family,' whispered Angus MacGregor. 'You know that, John. Ye ken fine what it's like.'

'Oh, don't leave, Angus,' cried Joseph. 'I'll take the beating for you. I'll say it was all my fault.'

Joseph turned white as he realized what he had just said.

He turned to escape from his new knight-errant self and bumped into Captain Hart. Joseph turned even whiter. He had said he would take the beating meant for Angus. He would need to stay.

'A word with you, Tregarthan,' barked the captain. 'In private, if you please.'

'Please, sir, Mr Hart, sir,' gabbled Joseph. 'It-wasallmehfault. I shall take the beating.'

'What, heh! Oh, the cook,' grinned the captain.

He threw a guinea on the table in front of the astonished MacGregor.

'Great pudding-faced harridan,' said the captain.

Then he began to laugh, a grating, rusty sound.

'Come along, Tregarthan,' he said.

'No beating?' quavered Joseph.

'No, lad. No beating.'

Joseph put both hands up to his mouth, mumbled something, and fainted dead away. Lord Tregarthan caught him before he hit the floor. The dining-room bell began to ring noisily. Lord Tregarthan eased Joseph onto the floor while Lizzie rushed from the scullery to sink down beside the footman and pillow his head on her lap.

'I don't understand,' said Mr Bullfinch. 'What is going on here? Family? Are they all related?'

'Better return to the dining room,' said Lord Tregarthan. 'What did you say to distress little Miss Jane?'

'She distressed me,' snapped Mr Bullfinch. 'A private matter.'

'Come along, Tregarthan,' said Captain Hart.

Upstairs, the guests had fallen silent. Alice and Jenny passed round the dishes. Mrs Hart was shaken. It was decidedly bad *ton* to have only female servants waiting at table. Where was Rainbird? And Joseph?

At last Rainbird appeared and, leaning over Mrs Hart, said, 'Captain Hart presents his compliments and says MacGregor is not to be either chastised or dismissed.'

Mrs Hart seethed inwardly. What had happened to the husband who used to obey her every whim?

Soon Mr Bullfinch returned and took his place beside Jane. Jane was suffering agonies of remorse. Where was Lord Tregarthan? Why did he not return? Summoning up her courage, she turned to Mr Bullfinch. 'Mr Bullfinch, I must explain what happened about . . . about the letters.'

'Yes?' said Mr Bullfinch, pushing away his plate. 'Go on.'

In a faltering voice, Jane described how she had become interested in the death of Clara, how the letters had been found by accident, and how she had read them to make sure they were not just old letters left in the desk by someone long ago.

'So having become convinced that I murdered my fiancée,' said Mr Bullfinch dryly, 'you quoted from one of my letters hoping to see me turn white with guilt.'

Jane hung her head.

'Return the letters to me and we shall say no more about the matter,' said Mr Bullfinch. 'I should never have accepted your mother's invitation, but a longing to be inside this house again, where I spent so many happy times with Clara, was too strong for me. It was a mistake.'

'But . . . but are you not *curious* as to how she died?' ventured Jane timidly.

'Can you not realize my agony on learning of her death, or how I closely questioned both doctor and coroner? And mine,' he went on bitterly, 'was not the idle curiosity of a spoilt child, but of a bereaved lover.'

Jane was being made to feel smaller and grubbier by the minute.

'I shall return your letters after dinner,' she said.

'And you will leave the matter alone?'

'Yes,' said Jane miserably.

Lord Tregarthan entered the room and, murmuring an apology to his hostess, took his place at table.

The dining-room door opened and Dave, the pot boy, popped his head round and signalled to Rainbird.

Rainbird left, only to return a few minutes later to call Joseph.

Mrs Hart set her lips. There had been enough fuss and scandal for one evening. She would *not* ask what was going on.

Conversation died. The sound of masculine voices came from outside the dining room, and then a grunting and panting and footsteps. Someone was carrying a heavy load past the door.

The guests had given up any pretence of making conversation. Everyone was listening to what was going on outside the room.

The street door banged and there was the rumble of carriage wheels outside.

Unable to bear it any longer, Mrs Hart rose, went to the window, and drew aside the curtains.

Rainbird and Joseph were strapping her husband's large sea trunk on to the back of a hackney.

The captain himself climbed into the carriage

and said something to Rainbird. The hackney moved off.

'What is it, mama?' asked Euphemia.

'Nothing,' said Mrs Hart, letting the curtain fall. 'Nothing at all.'

Afterwards, in the drawing room, Lord Tregarthan noticed Jane slipping quietly from the room.

She returned a few minutes later with a package of letters, which she passed to Mr Bullfinch, who seized them and thrust them into his pocket.

Lord Tregarthan wanted to speak to Jane to find out what had happened, but Mrs Hart commanded her to entertain the guests.

He joined her at the pianoforte and turned the music for her. She played indifferently, her fingers stumbling over the keys. At last, he covered one of her hands with his own and said quietly, 'Enough. You must tell me what is distressing you.'

Jane looked around quickly. Her mother was chatting to her guests, breaking off only to say good night to Mr Bullfinch. Euphemia was talking in a low tone to the Marquess of Berry.

Hanging her head, Jane mumbled her folly in baiting Mr Bullfinch with the contents of the letters.

'I shall speak to him,' said Lord Tregarthan. 'Do not look so distressed. We are become so absorbed in the mystery, we have forgot we are dealing with human beings with feelings. I am to blame as much as you. Come, smile at me, Jane. Mr Bullfinch will forgive you.'

Jane smiled at him tremulously. He caught his

breath, amazed at his sudden desire to protect her, to kiss the distress from her eyes.

'I cannot take you driving tomorrow,' he said quietly. 'We must talk further, but the conventions forbid me seeing you alone anywhere outside a carriage drive in the middle of the afternoon.'

Jane thought quickly. Mr Bullfinch's remarks still hurt. She longed for more reassurance.

'I shall be gone for two weeks at the very least,' he went on.

'I could meet you in the servants' hall when the guests have gone,' said Jane. 'Rainbird will not mind. He does not like my mother.'

'And neither does your father,' thought Lord Tregarthan, but he said aloud, 'When we all leave, count two hours from that time, and I shall come down by the area steps. Are you sure the servants will not talk?'

Jane shook her head. 'Rainbird will tell them not to.'

The guests had recovered their spirits. There was so much delicious gossip to pass on to the rest of society the following day – about Mrs Hart's scene with her cook, and her husband's mysterious disappearance in the middle of dinner. Lord Tregarthan waited until the end without talking to Jane again.

Downstairs, Rainbird relaxed in the kitchen with the other weary servants. A bottle of Mr Hart's best port went the rounds, and even Lizzie was told to leave the dishes and come and join them.

'Where is Felice?' demanded Rainbird suddenly.

'She said she was tired and was going to lie down until Mrs Hart needed her,' said Mrs Middleton. 'Oh, my! Madam is going to be in such a taking about the captain leaving. Did he say where he was going?'

Rainbird shook his head. 'Said if he didn't tell us, then we could truthfully say we did not know. Mrs Hart should have realized you can't bully a man like that forever. Most likely he's gone back to join the navy.'

'You was awfully lucky, Angus,' said Alice. 'A guinea instead of a whipping.'

'Mrs Hart's loss was our gain,' grinned Jenny. 'Never had such a magnificent supper.'

'I couldnae think o' leaving,' said MacGregor sadly. 'It was grand o' Lord Tregarthan to offer me a post.'

'I know you love us, Angus,' said Mrs Middleton, her eyes filling with sentimental tears.

'It wisnae that,' said the cook grumpily. 'Lord Tregarthan had a Frenchie in charge o' the kitchen and thon Abraham says he throws the pots around something terrible. If there's one thing I cannae stand, it's a man in the kitchen who does not know how to keep his temper.'

They all burst out laughing, except Joseph.

'You deserved a whipping, you great hairy thing,' he sneered.

'Which you would ha' taken for me,' grinned MacGregor. 'Aye, Joseph, you're no' the mamby-pamby I thought.'

'Mr Rainbird!'

They all rose to their feet as Jane walked in. How companionable they all were, she thought with a pang of envy. More like a real family than her own.

'I wish to speak to you, Mr Rainbird.'

Rainbird led the way into the servants' hall and inclined his head as Jane said she wished to be private with Lord Tregarthan.

'You may see him alone on one condition,' said Rainbird. 'The door to the servants' hall will be left open and I shall be on the other side of it, in the kitchen. But why on earth does his lordship wish to meet you here?'

'We wish to be private to talk for a little, that is all. *Please*, Mr Rainbird, I am too tired to go into long explanations.'

'Very well, miss,' said Rainbird. 'Don't keep me up too late.'

'Where is papa?'

'I do not know, Miss Jane,' said Rainbird. 'He left with his sea chest.'

'Does mama know?'

'Yes, but not where he has gone.'

'Is he *very* angry with mama?'

'That is not for me to say, Miss Jane.'

'Meaning, he *is*. Oh, dear. And where is Felice? I nearly forgot. Mama wants her to go upstairs and help prepare Euphemia for bed.'

'I shall call her. When is your assignation with Lord Tregarthan?'

'In two hours' time.'

'I shall be there, Miss Jane. How will he arrive?'

'By the kitchen door.'

Rainbird could hardly wait for her to leave so that he could go and see Felice. Since their night together at the play, they had not been alone. He ushered Jane out and, after telling the others of the secret meeting, went up the stairs and stopped on the landing outside Felice's door.

He scratched the panels. Then he called. There was no reply. She must have fallen asleep.

He gently opened the door and went in. A shaft of moonlight cut across the darkness of the room. Although the narrow bed in the corner was in darkness, he instinctively knew no one was in it.

There was a desolate, cold, *abandoned* air about the little room.

The fire was dying in the grate. He thrust a spill between the bars and lit a candle.

The bed was neatly made. A letter and a white packet lay on the pillow.

He felt a cold weight in his stomach as he put the candle down on a small table and picked up the letter and packet. The letter was addressed to himself, the packet to Joseph.

Downstairs, Joseph was playing the mandolin and the jaunty twanging music filtered up into the silence of the room.

Rainbird sat slowly down at the table and opened the letter. 'Dear John,' he read. 'I am gone to deal with a certain business which is my own concern. Thank you for all your kindness. Felice.'

And that was all.

Captain Hart, thought Rainbird, in sudden rage and fury. She had run off with Captain Hart. It must have happened when the captain spoke to her after the play. They must have arranged it then. And Felice with her gentle smile saying the captain had only required some translation of her!

Captain Hart. Old enough to be her father. It was disgusting!

Forgetting that Captain Hart was only a few years older than himself, Rainbird sat for a long time, his face a mask of tragedy.

Then he picked up the packet for Joseph and went downstairs.

Mrs Middleton looked up as he came in. Joseph saw the expression on the butler's face and his hands on the mandolin stilled.

'What is it?' asked Mrs Middleton.

'Felice,' said Rainbird. 'She's gone.'

He threw the packet in front of Joseph. 'She left that for you.' He hooked out a chair and slumped into it.

Joseph opened the packet and drew out a cambric handkerchief edged with the finest lace.

The Moocher jumped onto his lap and he patted him absent-mindedly. It was the most beautiful handkerchief Joseph had ever seen, but he would cheerfully have thrown it on the fire if he thought that action would manage to wipe some of the pain from Rainbird's face.

Lizzie voiced what they were all thinking. 'Did she run off with Mr Hart?'

'I don't know,' said Rainbird. 'Oh, God. Alice, answer that bell and tell Mrs Hart that Felice is unwell. I cannot bear any more scenes this evening.'

One by one they tried to cheer the butler up.

That was the French for you, sniffed Mrs Middleton. Fickle to the last woman.

Never could abide her, said Jenny, pouring a glass of port for Rainbird. But nothing seemed to help, and one by one they left, until Rainbird was alone, sitting at the table, nursing his heartache.

He sat there a long time until a knocking at the kitchen door reminded him of Lord Tregarthan's meeting with Jane.

Jane arrived by the back stairs at the same time, and Rainbird led them into the servants' hall and left them alone.

He felt wretched and bone weary. He did not care if Lord Tregarthan seduced Jane Hart on the table. With dragging steps he took himself off to bed, unaware that little Lizzie was lying awake on her pallet on the scullery floor, hugging the large cat and crying over the butler's pain.

TEN

. . . riding round those vegetable puncheons
Call'd 'Parks,' where there is neither fruit
or flower,
Enough to gratify a bee's slight munchings;
But, after all, it is the only 'bower'
(In Moore's phrase) where the fashionable fair
Can form a slight acquaintance with fresh air.

LORD BYRON, *DON JUAN*

'I came to say goodbye,' said Lord Tregarthan.

Jane's first thought was that he was abandoning her because of her disgraceful behaviour over the letters. He had appeared to understand, but gentlemen had such a rigid code of morals and mama always said they stuck together in the end. He had had time to consider her folly and had found her wanting in grace and manners. His sympathies were all with Mr Bullfinch.

'Goodbye,' said Jane, now wishing he would go away so that she might relieve some of the pain at her heart with a hearty burst of tears.

'So very prim,' he teased. 'Sit down, Jane, I have something to say to you. While I am gone you are to proceed no further with your investigations into Miss Clara Vere-Baxton's death.'

'Do you think I am in danger?' asked Jane, wide-eyed.

'I think you are in danger of making yourself ridiculous in the eyes of society. With luck, I found Mr Bullfinch at Brook's after dinner, nursing his woes, and was able to persuade him to forgive you. He sends you his apologies for any hard words he may have said to you. He said he was not quite himself, and visiting this house had opened old wounds. I gained the impression that Clara, despite Mr Bullfinch's worship of her memory, was not the innocent miss we had believed. From what Mr Bullfinch let drop unwittingly, it seemed the fair Clara delighted in tormenting him.'

Jane was about to say she had gathered as much from his letters, but decided it would be better not to remind Lord Tregarthan that she had read them. 'Are you going away?' she asked instead. 'Where are you going?'

He was silent for a moment, and then he said lightly, 'South.'

'Why?'

'I wish to visit a weaver who is supposed to have some very fine cloth. I shall look so dashing and handsome when I return, you will not recognize me.'

'Is that all you care for?' asked Jane. 'Your tailor? Your clothes? The Season?'

'I care for you, Jane,' said Lord Tregarthan, to his own surprise. 'I really do care for you.'

Jane's feelings shot from misery to exaltation at such a rate that she had to hang on to the table for support. She tried to remember Felice's teaching, which had included instructions on how gracefully to accept compliments from a gentleman you wished to encourage as well as how to repel unwelcome advances, but her mind was a blank. She hung her head and blushed.

She longed to look up at him, to discover whether he cared for her as a woman or whether he considered her a wayward schoolgirl, likely to land in trouble.

'I must go now,' he said gently. 'We should not be meeting in such an irregular way.'

'Yes,' said Jane politely, holding out her hand, while inside her a voice cried, 'I love you, please love me in return.'

He took her hand and raised it to her lips. She was still wearing her dinner gown and her head was bowed so that he could see only the roses in her hair. He put a finger under her chin and tilted her face up. Jane's large hazel eyes met his with such a blaze of love that he gave a muttered exclamation and pulled her tight into his arms and bent his mouth to hers.

All in an instant, Jane crossed the threshold into womanhood on a wave of searing passion. As his lips moved against her own, as his arms tightened even more about her, the churning mixture of sweetness and pain, longing and passion inside her made her utter a stifled cry.

Lizzie, lying awake on her pallet, heard the choked sound. She knew that Miss Jane and Lord Tregarthan were alone together in the servants' hall. She also knew that for some unaccountable reason Rainbird had left them unchaperoned. Lizzie tried to tell herself it was all none of her business, but even down in the kitchens she had heard of Lord Tregarthan's rakish reputation, and Miss Jane was so very young.

Lizzie decided that if she could get the Moocher to rush into the servants' hall, then she could race after it and break up whatever was going on. She gave the cat lying against her side an impatient push, but the Moocher had dined well, as well as the servants, on all the rich concoctions MacGregor had prepared and Mrs Hart had refused, and he growled impatiently and snuggled closer to Lizzie.

'No, you should not, my lord!' cried Jane suddenly and loudly as Lord Tregarthan's experienced fingers closed around one breast. Then she murmured huskily, 'Perhaps you should,' before turning her mouth up to his again.

Lizzie gritted her teeth. Her duty lay plain before her. She rose and pulled on a cotton wrapper over her shift and made her way into the servants' hall, coughing loudly and bumping into things to make as much noise as possible. When she opened the door, the couple were standing a little apart. Jane's mouth looked slightly swollen. Lord Tregarthan looked as unruffled as usual. 'I thought I heard a noise,' said Lizzie, dropping a curtsy.

'It is only us, as you see,' smiled Lord Tregarthan.

'Yes, my lord,' said Lizzie and stood her ground, which she felt was very brave of her. Lizzie had rarely seen any members of the Quality face to face. Usually she got an oddly angled view of them either looking up the area steps or looking down from Alice's and Jenny's room in the attic, as it was part of Lizzie's duties to clean the maid's room. There was something so terrifyingly magnificent about this handsome lord with the guinea-gold hair and the impeccable evening dress.

Lord Tregarthan gave Lizzie a mocking glance and then turned to Jane. 'I shall ask your father's permission to pay my addresses to you when I return,' he said. 'Goodnight, Jane.'

He raised his hand, picked up his hat and cane, and then he was gone.

Lizzie smiled with relief. Lord Tregarthan was going to marry Miss Jane, so all was well.

Jane moved past her like a sleepwalker and made her way out of the kitchen.

Lizzie went back to bed, pushing aside the cat, which was now stretched right across her mattress.

'It must be lovely, Moocher,' she whispered wistfully, 'to be allowed to fall in love and get married.'

Number 67 Clarges Street shook with a series of disasters the next day. Captain Hart had left and

Felice had left as well, and even the most thick-headed put one and one together and made two.

Joseph told Luke, the Charterises' footman, Luke told the upper servants clientele of The Running Footman, and so the news that Captain Hart had left his wife spread throughout the world – that is, the only world that mattered, St James's Square to Grosvenor Square. Who was Captain Hart, anyway? No one had thought to ask before, concentrating as they did on the 'originality' of Mrs Hart. Why, said one to another, Mr Nevill had said he was none other than the famous hero of the Nile and Trafalgar – *that* Captain Hart.

His wife had made him sell out and at last, after a long time of being nagged to death, he had turned and run off with the lady's maid and good luck to the man! By the time society had breakfasted on hot chocolate and risen from bed at two in the afternoon to face the rigours of a new day, Mrs Hart was socially damned. Originality became vulgarity in the eyes of the *ton*.

By four o'clock that afternoon Mrs Hart and Euphemia were dressed and prepared to receive callers, including the Marquess of Berry, who was to take Euphemia driving at five.

But no callers arrived. The Marquess of Berry sent a note to say he could not take Euphemia driving as he was otherwise engaged and, alas, was quite sure he would be otherwise engaged for some time. The Marquess had thought this a very delicately witty snub, but to Mrs Hart and Euphemia it was the cut direct.

More letters and cards arrived. Mrs Hart must understand that the invitation to this ball or that rout had been sent in error.

Unfortunately, Mr Brummell had met the Duchess of Devonshire the previous evening and had learned that the snuff box was not a present from Mrs Hart after all. He gleefully added his mite of gossip to the seething cauldron.

Then someone else said that Captain Hart had married beneath him and that Mrs Hart was none other than the daughter of a tenant farmer. Gracious! Society shuddered to think they had allowed such a person within their rooms.

By the time several people remembered that Mrs Hart had been an heiress and although she had made her come-out in Brighton, not London, she had been, and was, a member of the gentry, no one wanted to listen. The farmer's daughter story was much better.

Mrs Hart had a fit of the vapours and took to her bed. Euphemia, still confident in the power of her beauty, was convinced the whole scandal would soon blow over.

Only Jane was happy.

But even that was not to last very long.

Abraham, Lord Tregarthan's footman, had called to talk to Rainbird and admire Alice. During the conversation, he produced the note he had forgotten to deliver and laid it on the table. 'Better put it on the fire and forget about it,' said Rainbird.

'You do it for me,' said Abraham. 'I keep carrying it about, I don't know why.'

Heavy footsteps heralded the arrival of the agent, Jonas Palmer. Abraham took his leave. The servants immediately recollected pressing duties. Palmer interrogated Rainbird about the tenants. He had heard the gossip about Captain Hart leaving and wanted to know whether Mrs Hart planned to vacate the house. It might be possible to keep the Harts' money and rent the house to another tenant for the rest of the Season.

'Ask her yourself,' said Rainbird crossly.

'I'll do that,' said Palmer. 'And I'll have a talk to her about you. Seems to me you've been getting fat and lazy.' He rose to go. With an exclamation of annoyance, Rainbird went off to his pantry. Palmer saw the note addressed to Mrs Hart, picked it up, and carried it upstairs. Joseph was sent ahead to request Mrs Hart to see the agent.

But Mrs Hart sent down word that she was much too fatigued. Palmer left the note on the silver tray in the hall and left. Alice, seeing the note, thought it was a new one, as she was sure Rainbird had thrown that one from Abraham on the kitchen fire. She took it up to Mrs Hart, who was lying in bed, half drugged with laudanum.

Mrs Hart read it in amazement. It was marked Monday, the day before, but without a date. At least he had had the decency to state that his intentions were merely to discuss business with Captain Hart. He must be unaware of the fact that the captain had left.

But Jane had been going about with a dreamy

smile on her face – insulting to her mother, who felt Jane might at least show some natural feeling over the disappearance of her father, not knowing that Jane was too much in love to realize quite what was going on. The idea of bringing her strong-willed younger daughter down a peg was irresistible. Mrs Hart sent for Jane.

One look at the glowing happiness on her daughter's face was enough to tell Mrs Hart that Jane had again been misled by Beau Tregarthan. She heaved herself up against the pillows and fixed her daughter with a cold eye. 'Has Tregarthan been giving you the impression that he meant to call on Mr Hart with a view to asking permission to pay his addresses to you?'

'Yes, mama,' said Jane.

Something stabbed at Mrs Hart's never-too-active conscience. The girl looked beautiful, the shining, wonderful beauty of a woman who knows she is loved. But, like most miserable people, Mrs Hart wanted to spread the misery about.

'Then you are mistaken,' she said harshly. 'I have here a note from Lord Tregarthan in which he says his reason for calling on Mr Hart is purely to discuss a business matter. It is clear he thinks he may have given you the wrong impression.'

A dark shadow crossed Jane's face. 'May I see the letter, mama?'

Mrs Hart tossed it on the bedcover and Jane picked it up. A hot tide of shame washed over her. She had allowed him *such* familiarities; she would have allowed him more had not Lizzie appeared on the scene. With a choked sob, she crumpled up the note and fled from the room.

Jane longed for her father for the first time in her life. He would know what to do, of that she was sure. But he was gone, and there was no one else to turn to. She dared not ask Rainbird for advice, for that would mean telling the butler of her own shameful behaviour and she was sure Rainbird would be shocked.

So she nursed her grief to herself, longing for Beau Tregarthan to return so that she could tell him how much she despised and hated him. All Euphemia's nasty gossip about him burned in her brain.

For two whole days, the house in Clarges Street fell silent and became as shunned as it had been in previous years when the full weight of the bad-luck curse had been on it. Mrs Hart went into a decline, the last resort of a genteel lady making a bid for flinty-hearted society's charity.

Jane had cried until she could cry no more. But after the gloomy two days, the rainy weather, which had suited her mood, changed. Bright sunlight washed the London streets. And Mr Nevill came to take her driving in the Park. The fact that Mr Nevill was Lord Tregarthan's closest friend did not deter Jane from accepting his invitation. She felt she could not bear the mourning atmosphere of the house any longer. The full impact of her father's desertion had finally hit her. She could not in her heart of hearts blame him for leaving, only for disgracing them all by taking Felice.

Mr Nevill was an easy-going escort. He was blunt and direct and had none of the social graces of his friend. He quickly found out that Jane Hart was very good company provided Lord Tregarthan's name did not cross his lips, something that puzzled Mr Nevill greatly, for Lord Tregarthan had told him to keep an eye on Jane and had given out all the signs of a man deeply in love for the first time.

Euphemia was not left to mope in the house either. The reported size of her dowry was enough to encourage several gentlemen to brave society's disapproval, and although the Marquess of Berry was still absent, there were enough young men present to restore Euphemia's *amour propre.*

Mr Bullfinch divided his time between his work in the City and his social life in the West End. He stayed most nights at his club because it was often too late in the evening to face the journey back to his home in Streatham.

He was determined to find a wife. He was sure a marriage based on mutual appreciation and affection would be successful. Already Clara's ghost was becoming a pale wisp of a thing. The visit to Clarges Street had been a mistake. The love letters, the very sight of the place, had brought all his old obsession and agony racing back. So long as he stayed away from anything that might remind him of Clara, he was convinced he would soon forget her.

As if the Fates had decided to mock this decision, he found himself faced with Mr Gillespie, who was strolling down St James's Street just as Mr Bullfinch was emerging from Brooks's. Mr Bullfinch experienced that familiar surge of impotent fury he always felt on the rare occasions when he met the doctor. Of course Gillespie could not be blamed for failing to find the reason for Clara's death, but still. . .

'How fares the world, Bullfinch?' called Mr Gillespie cheerfully.

'Middling,' said Mr Bullfinch. 'Where are you bound?'

'I'm bound for the nearest chop house to find something to eat and then I am going to call on a Mrs Hart in Clarges Street.'

'I know the lady. What is wrong with her?'

'I have not yet seen her.'

Mr Bullfinch hesitated. 'Look,' he said awkwardly. 'Mrs Hart's youngest daughter, Jane, has been poking and prying into the death of Clara Vere-Baxton. Seems convinced it was murder. Do not encourage her. I have been extremely distressed already by her curiosity. She is very young and means no harm, but perhaps if she brings the matter up, you might dampen her interest.'

'Most certainly I shall,' said the doctor angrily. 'Her suspicions are an insult to my professional ability. Good day to you, Bullfinch!' The doctor walked off down the street in a temper, thumping his gold-topped cane against the paving stones as he went.

When the doctor called at Number 67 Clarges Street that afternoon, it was to find Mrs Hart lying in a darkened bedroom with the windows firmly closed. He had heard the gossip about Captain Hart leaving her and correctly, but privately, diagnosed an acute case of injured pride. He prescribed some brightly coloured innocuous pills and recommended that she should get as much fresh air and sunlight as possible. The parks, he said, were good places for a little daily exercise. Mrs Hart thought of hard eyes and hard faces staring at her in the Row, moaned, and turned her face into the pillow.

Mr Gillespie quietly left the room and said to Rainbird, who was waiting on duty outside the open door, that he would like to see one of the daughters, preferably the younger one, who might have more time than the elder to care for her mother. He had heard of Euphemia's great beauty and would have liked to see the girl for himself, but, on the other hand, an opportunity to talk to Jane Hart and stop her from harbouring stupid suspicions about the death of Clara was most important.

Rainbird led him down to the front parlour, served wine and biscuits, and went to fetch Jane.

Jane looked curiously at Mr Gillespie as she entered the room, Lord Tregarthan's description of 'a waiter with sore feet' leaping to her mind. He had a pleasant, deferential smile and manner, but his eyes were hot and angry and restless. He told Jane bluntly that he believed Mrs Hart to be perfectly well although her nerves were overset, adding it was imperative that Jane saw to it that her mother had plenty of fresh air and sunlight as well as a plain diet.

Jane said she would do her best.

Mr Gillespie surveyed her steadily. 'I have been in this house before,' he said.

'I know,' said Jane. 'You see, I heard all about Clara Vere-Baxton's death.'

'A great tragedy,' said Mr Gillespie. 'She was very young and very beautiful.'

'And you could not find any cause of death?' asked Jane eagerly.

'None whatsoever.'

'But there must have been *some* cause.'

'Not known to medical science, I assure you. May I point out to you that such matters are hardly the business of young debutantes.'

'You are impertinent.'

'I am merely telling you, you would be better to leave things you do not understand alone. I have attended His Majesty. It is not for you to cast doubts on my ability. I am ordering you here and now to put the matter out of your mind, or it will be the worse for you.'

Jane looked at him sharply. 'Are you *warning* me?'

'Yes, I am warning you,' said the much-goaded doctor. 'I gather you have already caused a great deal of distress to Mr Bullfinch. You are a very clumsy little girl,' he added with some venom.

Jane's temper flared. 'Let me tell you this, Mr

Gillespie,' she said coldly. 'I am convinced there was something strange about Clara's death and I will not rest until I have investigated the matter further.' She rang the bell and asked Rainbird to show the doctor out.

'Oh, how silly I am,' thought Jane when he had gone. 'I don't care a fig about Clara Vere-Baxton anymore. I only wish this terrible pain at my heart would go away.'

When Mr Nevill called a half hour later, Jane persuaded him to take Mrs Hart with them to the Park and then spent an exhausting hour abovestairs talking her mother into getting up and dressed.

At last Mrs Hart allowed herself to be helped into the open carriage. As she had painted circles under her eyes and put heavy white *blanc* on her face in order to win the doctor's sympathy, she indeed looked a figure of tragedy.

Once more she became an item of interest to the *ton.* After all, no one else in London had supplied such an amusing source of gossip as Mrs Hart and they had quite missed her. The stories of her wealth and genteel background quickly ousted the farmer's daughter one and she was gratified to receive many kind enquiries after her health.

On the following day, cards and invitations began to arrive again. Mrs Hart rallied amazingly. It all went to show that a husband was not of much use anyway.

ELEVEN

I confessed to my physician that there was something on my mind which agitated me so violently, that I could find no rest . . .

HARRIETTE WILSON'S MEMOIRS

The fact that Jane Hart had been told to leave the mystery of Clara alone, by Lord Tregarthan who had abused her innocence, and by Mr Gillespie whom she had taken in dislike, made her all the more determined to find out more about it.

With nothing but the occasional visits of Mr Nevill to occupy her mind, Jane once more set to work and badgered Rainbird for more information on the late Clara. All that Rainbird could add to what he had previously told her was that Clara had one female friend, a Miss Lucas, who was believed to be in London for her umpteenth Season. Despite the size of her dowry, she was considered exceeding plain and would not 'take'.

Jane, puzzled, said that Miss Lucas seemed an odd sort of friend for the beautiful Clara. Rainbird primmed his lips and said he thought Miss Clara enjoyed the contrast between her own looks and those of Miss Lucas. It was another little thing added to the list of things already stored in Jane's mind, which all added up to form one rather unpleasant character. This whetted her interest rather than otherwise. Now it appeared more and more as if Clara Vere-Baxton were just the type to get herself murdered.

Encouraged by what she began to believe to be Mr Nevill's courtship of Jane, Mrs Hart decided to take her to a party that evening in Queen Street. There was no need to buy her a new gown. The one she had worn for the dinner in the honour of the Marquess of Berry would do. Jane was well aware there was nothing of the lover in Mr Nevill's attentions and often wondered why he should seek her company so often, but she wished to go out in society to see if she could find Miss Lucas and so she did not say anything to make her mother think otherwise.

The party was given by a Mrs Grace Baillie in her curious apartments on the ground floor of an old-fashioned house in Queen Street. Mrs Baillie was good *ton* but not very rich. The rooms were small and ill-furnished and so she had hit upon a novel way of arranging them. All the doors were taken away, all the movables carried off, and the walls were covered with evergreens and set about with trees in pots, through the leaves of which peeped the lights of coloured lamps festooned with garlands of paper flowers. Passages, parlours, bedrooms, and cupboards were all adorned, and in various corners were surprises for the amusement of the visitors: a cage of birds, a stuffed figure in a bower, water trickling over mossy stones in an ivy-covered basin, a shepherdess in white muslin, a wreath, and a crook offering ices, a Highland laddie in a kilt presenting lemonade, a cupid with cake, a gypsy with fruit, along with many other contrived intricacies, which formed a sort of maze. It was called an Arcadian entertainment and the *ton* were so thrilled with it all that several wits were already sitting in corners composing verses in honour of the evening.

Jane wandered away from her mother and Euphemia and asked various people whether Miss Lucas was present. At last, a debutante said she had just seen Miss Lucas arriving and Jane threaded her way back through the maze of small rooms and passages towards the entrance. A few more enquiries and she found herself face to face with Miss Petronella Lucas. Miss Lucas had a long horse-like face and was wearing a girlish ensemble of muslin and pink roses, which accentuated the sallowness of her skin.

Unused to approaching strangers without a formal introduction and frightened of social censure – although surely it was not the same as approaching a *man* – Jane shyly said she was staying at Number 67 Clarges Street and that she had recently learned Miss Lucas had been a friend of the late Clara.

'My poor Clara,' said Miss Lucas with a little gasp. 'How I miss her! Come apart. I would like to talk about her. I have never had such a friend since.'

She drew Jane a little aside into a rustic bower where there was a bench. Both ladies sat down together. Miss Lucas began to talk . . . and talk. Jane listened in increasing disappointment. According to Miss Lucas's story, she, Miss Lucas, had been the belle of the Season and therefore confidante and adviser to the less fortunate Clara. The catalogue of Miss Lucas's virtues went on and on.

People passed to and fro behind them and in front of them through the forest effect created by the evergreens while Jane wondered how she could escape. Miss Lucas appeared to be all eyes and teeth and made Jane feel like that unfortunate wedding guest who was trapped by the ancient mariner.

At last, when Miss Lucas paused for breath, Jane said, 'But did Miss Vere-Baxton have any beau other than Mr Bullfinch?'

'Well, as to that,' said Miss Lucas, laying her finger alongside her nose in a most vulgar way, 'Clara told me in confidence that . . . oh, I have dropped my fan.'

'I think it fell under the seat,' said Jane, rising. She leaned across Miss Lucas to see if the fan had fallen on that side of the bench when something made her twist round and look over her shoulder. A hand, a very white hand with a large mole on it, appeared through the shrubbery behind the bench. The hand held a dagger. It stabbed viciously down exactly at the point where Jane's back would have been had she remained sitting.

Jane screamed and screamed.

Miss Lucas, not knowing what the matter was, but feeling that Jane was outdoing her in dramatics, began to scream as well. Soon they were surrounded by concerned faces.

Breathlessly Jane told them what had happened. After the initial shock and consternation, several of the gentlemen began to laugh and said it was no doubt another of Grace Baillie's entertainments.

Mrs Baillie was appealed to. Although she knew nothing about it, she quickly grasped that the idea of a mysterious hand with a dagger could only add a welcome Gothic note and enhance her reputation as a hostess. To do her justice, Miss Lucas's behaviour had convinced Mrs Baillie that both girls had been imagining things. So Mrs Baillie took the credit and Jane's insistence that someone had tried to kill her was pooh-poohed.

Then Mrs Baillie got one of her own footmen armed with a wooden dagger to leap out at people from corners and so there was nothing Jane could do but insist she was sure the attack on her had not been a hoax. There had been something so deadly about that thrusting steel – and the footman did not have a mole on his hand.

She became too frightened to think of anything other than getting home. In any case because Miss Lucas was now laughing at her own fright and making a mockery of Jane's screams to some bored listeners, she could not be encouraged to go on about Clara.

Jane wandered off in search of her mother. Mrs Hart was only too ready to leave. She had been at the far end of the rooms when Jane had been attacked and so did not know anything of her daughter's scene. The Marquess of Berry had cut her and Euphemia was sulking. Mrs Hart pronounced the evening sadly flat.

They made their way through the intricate passages towards the street door.

Jane looked back with a shiver, wondering who it had been who had attacked her. It was then that she saw Mr Gillespie and Mr Bullfinch standing in an ante room, their heads together. As she stared, they both looked up and saw her.

Mr Gillespie gave his triangular smile and Mr Bullfinch smiled as well. Jane tried to drop a curtsy but her legs were shaking too much. She stumbled after her mother out of the house.

Rainbird was waiting for them when they arrived home. 'A letter has arrived, delivered by one of Lord Tregarthan's servants,' he said, handing the sealed parchment to Mrs Hart.

She took it with the tips of her gloved fingers and looked at it disapprovingly. 'No doubt it is another letter explaining he is *not* about to propose to Jane,' she said crossly while Euphemia tittered. Jane blushed miserably and followed her mother and sister into the front parlour.

While Euphemia poured tea and complained about the Marquess of Berry, Mrs Hart crackled open the letter. She stared at it and then turned it over.

'Why, it is from Mr Hart,' she said faintly. She fumbled in her bosom for her quizzing glass while Jane carried a branch of candles and set it on a table beside her.

Mrs Hart read the letter slowly and then read it again with many 'bless-my-souls' until both Euphemia and Jane felt they would die from curiosity.

'All *most* irregular,' said Mrs Hart at last. 'Your father and Lord Tregarthan appear to have gone to France to rescue an English family' – she raised the letter and squinted at it through her glass – 'the Hambletons, from a prison in Rouen where they had been incarcerated by Napoleon's troops. It all had to be done in the greatest secrecy, which is why he says he was unable to tell me anything. They are at Dover, or rather, that is where Mr Hart sent this letter from. Felice went with them as interpreter. Baggage! Mr Hart stood by with a schooner on the coast while Lord Tregarthan went to rescue them. It seems they needed Felice to ask questions in the town and find out which of the guards would be most likely to accept a bribe. They were chased by Napoleon's troops and only escaped by a hairsbreadth.'

'Felice had no right to be so sly,' complained Euphemia. 'I would not take her back if I were you, mama.'

'She is not coming back,' said Mrs Hart. 'Lord Tregarthan has supplied her with a dowry and she has gone to live in Brighton. Pah! Paying off his mistress, no doubt.'

Jane looked at her mother in a kind of wonder. Could she, Jane Hart, possibly dislike her own mother? As Mrs Hart prattled on, reading the letter out loud over and over again, Jane remembered that interview with Lord Tregarthan in the kitchen. Now that she knew he had been on the brink of a perilous adventure rather than a journey to see his tailor, his behaviour began to seem as if it might contain more of the lover than the fop.

But Jane was afraid of hoping too much. Lord Tregarthan would surely now be more beyond her reach than ever. He would return a hero and be fêted and courted. Jane thought of Felice and felt a stab of jealousy that the lady's maid should be allowed to share the adventure.

And yet, taken up as she was with thoughts of Lord Tregarthan, wondering how she should treat him on his return – coldly, a dignified nod, or to a casual smile and a handshake? – she had not forgotten the mystery of Clara. Someone had tried to kill her at Mrs Baillie's. Someone who would try to kill again.

By next morning, Mrs Hart was planning a rout to celebrate the captain's return and Jane felt she could not bear her company any longer. She said she had the headache and wished to retire to her room. Mrs Hart looked at her sharply. 'You must remember that Mr Nevill is calling this afternoon to take you out, Jane.'

Jane was almost on the point of saying she did not want to see Mr Nevill, but then she thought that Mr Nevill would know the hour of Lord Tregarthan's return, and Jane had a longing to see him, to look into his eyes and see whether he cared for her just a little. As she went out of the dining room, she met Rainbird, who was coming down the stairs from the attics. She gave him a faint smile and said, 'Well, Mr Rainbird, it appears my father is to return to us soon.'

Rainbird clutched the bannister. 'And Felice?' he asked.

'Not Felice,' said Jane. 'She is to be an independent lady with a dowry. Oh, I see you know nothing about it.' She told him the contents of her father's letter.

'Did Felice write? Did she mention me?' asked Rainbird.

'No,' said Jane. 'Were you expecting a letter?'

Rainbird shook his head sadly. 'No, of course not.' He went slowly down the stairs. It was some time before he could bring himself to tell the rest of the staff the news.

The first thing that Mr Nevill said after he drove off with Jane that afternoon was that he had received a letter from Lord Tregarthan.

'Really?' said Jane with affected indifference. He had not written to *her*. Why should he? Once more, her hopes sank. She had been an amusing diversion, nothing more.

At last Mr Nevill noticed her sad eyes and asked her if she were feeling unwell.

'No,' said Jane curtly.

Mr Nevill reined in his horses under a tree and looked at her anxiously. 'You can talk to me, you know,' he said.

Jane could not tell him of her love for Lord Tregarthan, but she suddenly felt she could tell him about her other fears. She poured out the whole story of Clara, of the party in Queen Street, and of that hand holding a dagger.

Mr Nevill heard her out in silence. Then he removed his curly-brimmed beaver and scratched his head in perplexity. 'You say both Bullfinch and Gillespie were there? But they are both highly respected gentlemen. I mean, you don't get a City banker or one of the King's doctors going around stabbing young ladies?'

'The trouble is,' said Jane, 'that people are always blinded by rank and position. If Mr Gillespie and Mr Bullfinch were Mr Bloggs and Jones of Hungerford Stairs, mudlarks by profession, everyone would cry, "Jane, one of them did it. Seize the villains!"'

'Why don't you discuss the matter further with Tregarthan?' asked Mr Nevill. 'Marvellous head on his shoulders. He should be with you tomorrow at the latest.'

'I do not know whether I want to see him again,'

said Jane in measured tones. 'I have not made up my mind.'

'Here, you can't say that!' said Mr Nevill angrily. 'I've been calling on you and squiring you around just so's no one else could whisk you away. He told me to look after you. Besides, he said he was looking forward to seeing you and I'm blessed if I know what he'll say to me when I tell him you don't want to see him.'

Jane took a deep breath. 'Lord Tregarthan mentioned me in his letter?'

'Yes, I have it here.' He fumbled in his many pockets and at last produced a crumpled piece of paper. 'Here we are . . . let me see . . . "curst bad crossing, Felice sick, captain sailed like Neptune" . . . ah, I have it. "All I want to do is see my little Jane as soon as possible. I hope you have taken good care of her." There!'

'So *that* is why you have been so kind,' said Jane, her eyes like stars.

'Of course it is. You didn't think . . . I mean, not that you ain't a pretty companion, it's just . . . Oh, I *say!*' For Jane had leaned forward and kissed him on the cheek.

'I did often wonder, Mr Nevill,' said Jane, 'why you called on me so much. I did not know until last night that Lord Tregarthan had gone off with my father to save that family in France. He . . . he told me he was going to see his tailor in the south country,' laughed Jane. 'Before he left, he told me to leave the mystery of Clara's death alone.' She clasped her hands, her eyes shining. 'But would it not be wonderful if I could manage to find out who killed her *before* his return?'

'No,' said Mr Nevill, looking alarmed. 'It all sounds a hum to me, daggers and bodies. Why don't you go home and get some rest. Tregarthan will be with you very soon.'

Jane smiled and nodded, but the happiness that had flooded her brain when she had learned of Tregarthan's desire to see her again seemed to have cleared it. She was sure if she sat down with pencil and paper and wrote down all she knew, then she might arrive at the correct solution.

When they returned to Glarges Street, Mr Nevill refused her offer of refreshment and drove off. Jane found her mother in the front parlour. 'Mr Gillespie called when you were gone, Jane,' she said. 'What is all this about you throwing an hysterical scene at Mrs Baillie's? There is some story going the rounds that you claimed someone had tried to stab you. It is making me look quite ridiculous, for you said nothing of it to me. Someone told me last night that a couple of females had started screaming at one of Mrs Baillie's novelties.'

'I made a mistake, mama,' said Jane. 'My nerves are a trifle overwrought.'

'That is what Mr Gillespie said and he kindly left some pills with instructions that you should take them and go to bed for the rest of the day. Really, Jane, I am your mother, or had you forgot? It seems incredible you should believe an attempt had been made on your life and say nothing of it to me.'

'I am sorry,' said Jane. 'I felt very silly when Mrs Baillie explained the whole thing had been a hoax.' Jane did not want to tell her mother of her suspicions or of the news that Lord Tregarthan cared for her after all. All her mother would do would be to trot out all the old scandals about the beau's love life and the futility of Jane nourishing any hopes in that quarter.

'I should have known better than to take you out anywhere,' said Mrs Hart fretfully. 'Does Nevill show any signs of proposing?'

'No, mama.'

'Well, I am not surprised. You are looking quite hagged. I must say there was a while when you looked very well. You are too intense, Jane. Excess of emotion can be very unflattering.'

Jane thought again about Lord Tregarthan, about how he had asked Mr Nevill to look after her, and another sunburst of happiness flushed her face and brightened her eyes.

'And you look feverish,' said Mrs Hart. 'Take your pills. You are to take two right away.' She poured a glass of water. 'Take them and go and lie down.'

Jane looked at the two pills lying on her mother's out-stretched hand. They were as red as rubies.

Jane slowly took them from her mother's hand. 'I shall take them in my room,' she said slowly.

But once in her room, she laid the pills on a clean piece of paper, drew forward another sheet of paper and began to write down everything she had discovered about Clara and about the events at Mrs Baillie's. She gave a little shiver and then rang the bell and asked Jenny, who answered its summons, to fetch Rainbird. Rainbird came in, looking curiously at Jane's white and rigid face. 'Sit down, Mr Rainbird,' said Jane. 'There is something I must tell you, and then there is something you must do for me.'

'I am going to fetch Mr Gillespie to examine Miss Jane,' said Rainbird some time later to Mrs Hart.

'Very well,' said Mrs Hart.

'Do you not wish to see her?' asked Rainbird.

'Well . . . I am sure it is nothing serious. Jane is a very resilient girl. You will find me at Mrs Baillie's at six o'clock should there be any cause for concern.'

'Selfish woman,' muttered Rainbird as he made his way out and along Clarges Street. Although he blamed Captain Hart more than Lord Tregarthan for supplying the means by which Felice had been able to secure her freedom from service – for if Captain Hart had not taken Felice away, she would still be in Clarges Street – he still liked and admired the man and felt he was a fool to return to such a querulous and domineering wife.

As soon as the captain returned, Rainbird planned to ask for a few days' leave. He was sure if he were to travel to Brighton and see Felice, he might be able to persuade her to marry him. He would need to find work outside of service where Palmer could not touch him, but somehow they would manage. Rainbird was too obsessed with Felice to worry overmuch about the fate of the other servants at Number 67. Love gave him mad hope. He was convinced that he would not only be married to Felice but also that somehow Mr Hart might help him find posts for the others.

Mr Gillespie was at home. As soon as Rainbird told him about Jane, he said they must make all speed. He was so white and tense that Rainbird had the impression he had been waiting for hours for such a summons.

Mr Gillespie mounted the stairs two at a time to Jane's bedchamber. But when he was outside the door, he hesitated, and then turned to Rainbird, who was right behind him. 'Mrs Hart, and Miss Euphemia, are they at home?'

'No, sir. They are at Mrs Baillie's.'

'I shall examine Miss Jane in privacy,' said Mr Gillespie. 'Leave me alone with her. Do not come near, no matter what you hear. Young ladies can become very nervous during examinations and I feel a *crise des nerfs* has distorted Miss Jane's wits. She is best left alone with her doctor.'

'Perhaps Mrs Middleton should be in attendance?' suggested Rainbird.

'No, no,' said Mr Gillespie heartily, clapping Rainbird on the shoulder. 'Do not look so worried, man. There is a great deal of fever about. That may be the cause of her disorder. None of you should risk catching it.'

He waited until Rainbird had gone down the stairs and then he went into Jane's bedchamber and shut the door.

The curtains were drawn and the light was dim. She lay propped up on her pillows, her eyes wide and dark in the gloom.

'Now let me have a look at you,' he said.

He walked towards the bed, stripping off his dogskin gloves as he did so. His hands were white, strong, and well-shaped.

On the right hand, there was a large mole.

Jane stared at it, and drew a long breath.

'You,' she said.

'It was you.'

TWELVE

See how love and murder will out.

WILLIAM CONGREVE, *AMORET*

Mr Gillespie stood very still, looking down at her.

Although her face was pale, she did not look ill in the slightest.

'You did not take the pills I left for you,' he said in a flat voice.

'I had them examined at the apothecary's in Curzon Street,' said Jane. 'They contained a very strong measure of quinine – enough to make me appear as if I had the fever. Mama would have sent for you.'

'So you sent for me instead, you meddling jade.' He drew a pistol from his pocket and levelled it at her. 'Don't scream,' he said.

'Why did you do it?' asked Jane, marvelling at the steadiness of her own voice.

'Why did I try to kill you at that Baillie woman's ridiculous party?'

'No,' said Jane. 'I know now that was you and you tried to kill me to stop me finding out how Clara died. I meant, why did you kill *her*?'

He sighed, sat down on the bed, and laid the pistol on his knee.

'She played me false,' he said. 'She played me false,' he repeated, and then fell silent.

A wheezy barrel organ was playing in the street below, a child called, a horse clopped past – all the sounds of everyday living came to Jane's ears while she pressed back against the pillows and faced the murderer of Clara Vere-Baxton.

'Why?' asked Jane again.

'She had a fever,' he said. 'I attended her. She told me she did not want to marry Bullfinch but that her parents were forcing her to accept him. I believed her. She was so very beautiful, the fragile beauty of a Dresden figurine. I fell deeply in love with her. I attended her several times.

'My love appeared to be returned. How could I think otherwise when, after her illness was over, she called at my rooms and became my mistress? I begged her to allow me to speak to her father, elope with me, anything so that she might become my bride.

'But she would cry. She could cry beautifully,' he said in a sort of wonder. Jane shifted in the bed and he slightly raised the pistol. 'She had very blue eyes and the tears would spill over and run down her cheeks without ever making her eyes red. She begged me to wait. That Lucas creature was party to our affair. Or rather, she knew Clara was seeing someone. I called on Miss Lucas this morning to be sure she still did not know it was me.' He laughed. 'She did not . . . and as well for her that she is ignorant of my part in things. When I saw and heard her talking to you last night, I was afraid she did know. Hence the attempt on your life. But to return to Clara,' he went on in a dreadfully normal conversational tone. 'She begged me to wait, as I said. When Clara was with me, she was always supposed to be with Miss Lucas.

'Then her visits stopped. I went wild with despair. One day she came to see me again. She had become hard. She told me Bullfinch had taken her to his bank. "It was lovely to be surrounded by so much money," she said, and she laughed.

'When I reminded her of our great love, Clara shrugged and said she had decided to marry Bullfinch after all. She meant to have a little more freedom and fun before then. She said it was *fun* to torment Bullfinch, and then I knew she had been his mistress also, and that she thought it was fun to make me suffer as well. Although I saw her at last for what she was – a scheming, heartless, vain jade – I could not stop loving her. But no one else was going to have her if I could not.

'As I watched her, I hit upon a plan. I pretended to take her rejection of me easily and lightly. I began to talk about my work. I said I had discovered a formula for prolonging youth. She was very naive and stupid. She begged me to give her some. Although she was very young, she had a terror of losing her looks. I gave her a heavy sleeping draught, and, when she was asleep, I smothered her with a cushion.'

'But she was found in the Green Park. She had gone out for a walk – that was what they said,' exclaimed Jane.

'Clara was supposed to have gone for a walk that afternoon when she was, in fact, with me. I wrapped her body in a blanket, went out by the back door of my house and into the mews. I suppose I could have been seen, but I was so mad with grief, I half wanted to be found out, and was at the same time just as determined to get away with it. Odd.

'I put her body on the floor of my carriage, harnessed up the horses myself. The minute Clara had arrived, I had sent all my servants off for the afternoon. My groom had fortunately understood that to mean himself and was nowhere around.

'I drove straight into the Green Park and stopped by the top reservoir. I opened the carriage door and jerked the blanket so that Clara's body rolled out onto the grass. She lay looking up at the sky. She looked very peaceful. A warden came rushing up and demanded to know what I was doing driving my carriage over the grass. I showed him Clara's body and said it had been reported to me and I had been summoned direct.'

'I did not know *you* were supposed to have found the body,' said Jane.

'In all the shouting and commotion that followed,

it was understood that the watch had called at my home and that the body had been discovered by an old woman. When the fuss died down, no one knew I had been there first, so to speak. I performed the autopsy myself, a distasteful business. No one questioned my findings, or lack of them.'

He fell silent again.

'You are a monster,' whispered Jane.

'Not I,' he said. 'Oh, not I. Blame this so-called London society, if you must blame anyone. I came from a poor family and worked my way up. I was a surgeon's mate, working in filthy ships from Portsmouth to the Americas. I was lucky enough to find myself a rich patron and to set up a practise in the West End.

'I rose rapidly. I knew how to flatter and cajole these useless hulks of society with their imagined humours. A solid day's work would cure most of them. But always behind their eyes, I saw their carefully veiled contempt. I would never be in society, only acceptable so long as I held the Duchess of Vanity's pulse and told her of her delicate constitution. Clara pointed this out to me. Mr Bullfinch has a great deal of money. Bankers, like brewers, are good *ton.* Doctors are not.

'Now, you, had you more to occupy your silly mind, then you would not meddle in other people's affairs.'

'Are you going to kill me?' asked Jane.

'But of course,' said Mr Gillespie.

'Of course.'

* * *

Lord Tregarthan tossed off his muddied travelling clothes and splashed his head and shoulders with hot water while his friend, Mr Nevill, watched him in a bemused way. 'I thought you were going to wait until morning to call on Miss Jane,' he said.

'Not after what you told me,' said Lord Tregarthan, scrubbing himself dry with a towel.

'What? About that Clara business? Oh, you know gels do have a lot of imagination. Take it from me, it's all a hum.'

'I never thought it a hum,' said Lord Tregarthan, pulling on a frilled cambric shirt. 'I told her to drop the whole thing because I feared any further investigations might put her at risk. She may even now be in danger.'

'It must be love,' said Mr Nevill with wonder. 'You'll meet and kiss and you will both have a good laugh at your wild imaginings.'

'I hope so,' he said grimly.

'Ain't you going to ring for your valet?'

'No, he'll take too long.'

Mr Nevill watched in admiration as his friend scrambled into his evening clothes at top speed. 'Want me to come with you?' he asked.

'No,' said the earl with a grin. 'I want her all to myself.'

But as Lord Tregarthan walked to Clarges Street, he put away his fears for Jane's safety, and concentrated instead on the joy of seeing her again.

The door to Number 67 stood ajar. He walked

into the hall and found Alice, Jenny, Lizzie, and Mrs Middleton huddled at the foot of the stairs. They turned and looked at him, their eyes showing a mixture of excitement and fear. 'Where is Miss Jane?' he asked.

'She is upstairs being attended by Mr Gillespie . . .' began Mrs Middleton, but Lord Tregarthan did not wait to hear any more. He bounded up the stairs and almost fell over Rainbird, who was sitting on the landing outside Jane's bedchamber, holding a cudgel. He put his finger to his lips when he saw the beau. 'I'm waiting for the signal,' he whispered.

Lord Tregarthan was about to demand, 'What signal?' when there came an unearthly blood-curdling shriek from Jane's bedroom.

Rainbird leapt to his feet.

'That's it!' he cried.

Holding the pistol steady, Mr Gillespie edged closer to Jane. Behind him, the door of a large wardrobe slowly swung open revealing Angus MacGregor, Dave, and Joseph. Unaware of their presence and that they were waiting to spring, Mr Gillespie inched even closer while Jane crouched back against the pillows.

'You cannot shoot me,' said Jane. 'If you shoot me, then everyone will know it was you.'

'True,' he said. 'But there are better ways . . .' He suddenly jerked the pillow out from behind Jane's head and brought it down with murderous force over her face.

MacGregor's Gaelic warcry sounded behind him as if all the demons had risen from hell to claim his soul.

At the same moment, the door of the bedroom burst open and Lord Tregarthan dashed in with Rainbird.

Mr Gillespie disappeared in a tangle of arms and legs and MacGregor, Dave, and Joseph threw themselves on top of him on the bed.

He wriggled out from under them like an eel, fell onto the floor, and scrabbled for his pistol. Lord Tregarthan stamped on his groping hand and Miss Jane Hart, with a triumphant cry, brought a full jug of water down on the doctor's head.

He stretched his length on the floor and lay still.

'Get the watch! Get the constable!' cried Lord Tregarthan.

He picked Jane up bodily from the bed and cradled her against his chest, smoothing back the tumbled hair from her eyes.

'You are brave and crazy,' he said. 'Why on earth did you allow that fellow near you, you with all your suspicions?'

Jane smiled at him mistily. 'I wanted to be brave as well. I wanted to be worthy of you, and I thought I would be wonderful to catch the murderer of Clara myself. The servants agreed to help. They were told to hide in the wardrobe until he had betrayed himself and then rush to the rescue.'

'But we couldnae rush when we wanted,' said MacGregor, 'because he had the gun and we were feart it might go off.'

Mrs Middleton, Alice, Jenny, and Lizzie all crowded into the room. Jane only had eyes for Lord Tregarthan. 'I thought you did not love me,' she said shyly.

He bent his head and kissed her, kissed her the way he had dreamed of kissing her all those weary days in France. He felt her passion rise to meet his own and all his fears that she might be too young, innocent, and frightened to match his feelings melted away. He was too much lost in the feel of her, in the scent of her, and the sharp awareness that she was wearing nothing other than a thin muslin nightgown to notice the staff of Clarges Street gathered around, gazing at the pair of them with silly smiles on their faces, except for Dave, who went very red about the ears and started making wretching noises until Mrs Middleton cuffed him.

Mr Gillespie, who had recovered consciousness some moments before, startled them by leaping to his feet and making a dash for the door.

He made it as far as the landing when Rainbird's cudgel struck him full across the shoulders.

He toppled straight over the bannisters and fell down the stairwell like a stone. He struck his head on the tiles of the hall and lay still.

After seemingly hours of questions and hysterics while Number 67 Clarges Street resounded to the tread of alien feet from the Bow Street Runners to every reporter in town, including a woman of stultifying gentility who wrote the Home News column in *The Lady's Magazine*, Lord Tregarthan managed to see Jane settled for the night and requested an audience with Mrs Hart.

Mrs Hart eyed the handsome beau with disfavour. On her arrival back, his comments on her neglect of her younger daughter had been caustic to say the least. 'It is now two in the morning, my lord,' she said frostily. 'I would remind you of that fact. I am not made of iron, you know. My poor Euphemia is quite overset.'

'Poor Euphemia has not as much to be upset about as Jane,' he said coldly. '*She* was not half killed.'

'But she has the greater sensibility,' said Mrs Hart tartly. 'And *when* may I expect my husband's return?'

'He has decided not to return, madam. He has rejoined the navy and is awaiting his ship in Dover. He is anxious to be of service to his country. By Gad, madam, Captain Hart is a Trojan, and this nation is lucky to have him.'

Mrs Hart raised a wisp of handkerchief to her lips. '*Not* returning. But he must! I have already sent out invitations to a rout in his honour.'

Lord Tregarthan looked at her in exasperation. Her daughter had been nearly murdered, a murderer had been found with his neck broken in her hall, and yet all she could think about was her blasted party.

'Before I left Captain Hart,' he said, 'I told him I wished to marry your daughter and received his permission.'

'Not Jane?'

'Of course, Jane.'

Mrs Hart studied him. All at once she hated this handsome lord who had been instrumental in luring her husband away from her, who had spoiled the social triumph of her planned rout, who had dared to rail at her over her treatment of Jane. A slight tinge of malice crept into her pale eyes. 'Jane is too young to know her own mind,' said Mrs Hart.

Lord Tregarthan looked at her, outraged. 'Does that mean you withhold your permission?'

'Yes,' said Mrs Hart. 'Yes, I do. And since Captain Hart chooses to behave like an unnatural husband and father by holding himself absent, he no longer has any say in the matter.'

'*You* are the unnatural parent, not he,' raged Lord Tregarthan.

Mrs Hart experienced a slight qualm of unease. Lord Tregarthan was a Catch. It would be folly to refuse his offer. But let him sweat a little. He must be punished for having said all those hard things.

'As I told you,' she said in a deceptively mild tone, 'Jane is very young. Perhaps if you are prepared to wait a few years . . . ?'

'Good evening, madam,' said Lord Tregarthan in tones of deepest disgust.

'But . . .' Mrs Hart realized she had gone too far and half rose from her seat, but Lord Tregarthan was already striding from the room.

He made his way angrily down Clarges Street, determined to see Jane in the morning and try to discover what they could do. Mr Hart had given his permission, but not in writing. Perhaps it might be necessary to go back to Dover and ask Mr Hart to delay sailing and to travel to London to see his daughter wed. But he was back in the Royal Navy and it was highly unlikely he would be allowed to do so.

Lord Tregarthan heard the light patter of feet behind him, and swung around, stick at the ready in case it should prove to be a footpad. But the dim light of the parish lamp shone down on the features of Rainbird.

'My lord,' said Rainbird, 'when does Captain Hart return?'

'He does not,' said Lord Tregarthan. 'I have just been explaining to Mrs Hart that Mr Hart has rejoined the navy.'

Rainbird's face fell. 'I had hoped, my lord, to ask Mr Hart's permission to take some days' leave of absence. You see,' he burst out, 'I must see Felice. We had an understanding . . .'

'I am sorry,' said Lord Tregarthan gently. 'I did not know.'

'She said nothing of me?'

'Felice was sea sick and then too worried about the perils of our mission to talk about anything else. She never said anything about herself, other than that her parents had been servants in a noble French household and had fled to England when their masters were killed. They died a short time ago and Felice went into service.'

'If I could only see her,' said Rainbird, twisting his hands.

'I shall give you her direction. She has friends in Brighton and has gone to stay with them.'

'But how am I to get away?' asked Rainbird.

Lord Tregarthan stood in thought. 'You might simply leave and then come to me afterwards if you need another post.'

'Thank you, my lord, but if Felice will have me, I must find another type of work. If she does not, then I would like to return to the others.'

Lord Tregarthan nodded, understanding the 'others' to mean that odd 'family' of servants at Number 67.

'I will help you, Rainbird,' he said at last, 'if you will do something for me. Tell Mrs Hart that I told you Captain Hart wished you to travel to Dover to collect a present for his wife. She is greedy and vain and will let you go. She needs something to show the world that her husband still cares for her. I will furnish you with such a present.'

'Thank you, my lord.'

'In return, I want you to bring Miss Jane to my house at three o'clock tomorrow afternoon. I do not want her mother to see her leave.'

'Yes, my lord. Mrs Hart often goes out of an afternoon and leaves Miss Jane alone.'

'Very well. Come closer under the light so I may write out all the instructions for you.'

'And Felice's address?'

'And Felice's address.'

THIRTEEN

O Lord, sir, when a heroine goes mad she always goes into white satin.

RICHARD BRINSLEY SHERIDAN, *THE CRITIC*

Jane Hart was puzzled and worried.

She had slept late, dressed, and rushed downstairs to accept her mother's congratulations on a successful alliance with Lord Tregarthan. But Mrs Hart and Euphemia were both gone from the house.

Jane rang and asked Joseph, who answered the bell, the whereabouts of her mother and whether Lord Tregarthan had called. Joseph said he did not know where Mrs Hart had gone, Rainbird might know but he was out on an errand, and no one had called except persons from the law and persons from the newspapers, all of whom he had sent away.

'Mr Rainbird will be leaving us for a few days,' said Joseph with a self-important air. 'I am in charge until his return, so if there is anything you wish, please let me know.'

'Send Mr Rainbird to me when he returns,' said Jane.

Joseph bowed his way out – in quite the royal manner – and spoiled the effect by knocking over a spindly chair.

Jane paced up and down. If Lord Tregarthan had told her mother that she, Jane, was to wed him, then surely that mother should have been waiting, overjoyed with such good news. Jane stopped in front of the looking glass and studied her appearance. Could such a woman as herself attract a man like Tregarthan? Although she looked very modish in one of Euphemia's gowns, which had been altered for her by Felice, she had to admit she could find little about her face or figure to charm a famous beau.

If only she were a man then she could simply walk around to his home and see him. But, of course, if she were a man, she would not be so terribly in love.

Jane walked to the window and looked out into Clarges Street. People were emerging from the house opposite, the house where the great Charles James Fox had lived and died. Who were they? wondered Jane idly. What a strange place London was, where one could live cheek by jowl with so many people and yet not know them. Mrs Hart had invited Lady Charteris next door to tea, but Lady Charteris seemed determined not to know Mrs Hart whether that lady were in fashion or out of it.

Then Jane saw Rainbird walk past, clutching a

large parcel. She ran to the front door and opened it. 'Mr Rainbird,' she called. 'Oh, Mr Rainbird, I am so glad to see you. No one is here and I don't know where mama is, and Lord Tregarthan has not even called.'

Rainbird stepped past her and placed the wrapped box on a chair. 'I am to take you to Lord Tregarthan's home in Brook Street at three o'clock,' he said in a low voice. 'It is as well Mrs Hart is not here. Lord Tregarthan wishes you to leave without anyone but myself knowing about it. I am to leave you there and then I, myself, am making a short journey.'

'What is it all about?' asked Jane.

'I do not know, miss. Those were my instructions – to escort you there.'

Jane twisted about and looked at the clock in the hall. 'It is half past two,' she cried, 'and I must change my gown, and . . . and . . . I have not eaten. Never mind, I shall do as he says.'

'Meet me here, Miss Jane, in fifteen minutes,' said Rainbird.

Jane nodded and flew up the stairs to her room to look out her best gown and bonnet. She no longer cared why he wanted to see her, only that he *did* want to see her.

Rainbird went downstairs to the kitchens. He deposited the parcel on the table. 'Hide this,' he said to Mrs Middleton, 'and if I do not return, give it to Mrs Hart and say it is a present from the captain. Should I return, then I will give it to her myself.'

Mrs Middleton's eyes filled with tears. 'I never thought the day would come, Mr Rainbird,' she sobbed, 'when you would leave us all for some French hussy.'

'Hush,' said Rainbird gently. 'I told you all this morning that after I marry Felice and get established, I will try to find a way of bringing us all together again.'

'*I* wouldnae leave,' said the cook. 'You know that. How can you do this?'

'I am very much in love,' said Rainbird simply, and only Lizzie saw the pain in Mrs Middleton's eyes.

'Don't worry,' said Joseph, strutting up and down. 'I shall take care of you all.'

'That's what worries me,' said the cook gloomily.

'I am leaving now,' said Rainbird, 'and I am taking Miss Jane somewhere before I catch the Brighton coach. But you are to know nothing of that. Simply say you do not know when Miss Jane left.'

They lined up by the kitchen door as he picked up his portmanteau. He looked at them all, his eyes filling with tears. He shook hands with Joseph, then Angus and then Dave, the pot boy. He embraced Mrs Middleton, Jenny, and Alice. He turned to Lizzie, who was looking up at him with large reproachful eyes. 'Forgive me, Lizzie,' said Rainbird. 'You alone should know why I must go.'

Lizzie began to cry, and he held her closely against him and then kissed her cheek. All of them were now in tears, MacGregor howling like a banshee, Dave scrubbing his eyes with his fists, and Joseph sobbing into the lace handkerchief Felice had made for him.

Rainbird strode up the stairs, his heart heavy. Even the thought of seeing Felice again could not seem to lighten the pain. Jane was too happy and excited to notice the strain on Rainbird's face. Rainbird called a hack, and they travelled in silence to Brook Street.

Jane's heart sank a little as she stood on the doorstep of Lord Tregarthan's home. Rainbird sounded a brisk tattoo on the knocker.

Outside on the road stood a travelling carriage with a bewigged coachman up on the box. Two postillions in green jackets and jockey caps waited alongside. 'Is that Lord Tregarthan's carriage?' asked Jane nervously.

'I believe it is,' said Rainbird.

He is going back to the army, thought Jane miserably. He is going to say goodbye to me and that will be that.

The door opened.

'Goodbye, Miss Jane,' said Rainbird. He hesitated. 'If you are ever in a position of consequence as a married lady, please do not forget the staff at Number 67. They would be glad of references.'

Lord Tregarthan's butler gave Rainbird a steely glare and ushered Jane inside.

'Of course I shall,' called Jane. 'Tell them I shall

not forget them. In fact I shall tell them so myself this very evening.'

Rainbird lifted his hand in farewell as the Tregarthan butler shut the door. Lord Tregarthan came out of the library to meet her and raised both his hands to her lips. His butler, Welks, stood to attention in a corner of the hall, awaiting orders.

'Are you ready?' asked Lord Tregarthan.

'For what?' asked Jane. 'What is happening?'

'We are eloping, my little love. Come, I can tell you all about it on our journey to Gretna.'

'Elope!' shrieked Jane. 'I am not prepared. I have no clothes . . .'

He silenced her with a kiss. Welks looked at the ceiling and wondered what the world was coming to. Imagine behaving in such a scandalous way before your very own butler.

'Don't you want to come with me?' asked Lord Tregarthan.

'Oh, my lord,' cried Jane, stretching up on tiptoe to throw her arms around his neck. 'I would go to the ends of the earth with you.'

'No, only to Gretna Green for a Scotch marriage.'

He put his arm around her and led her out of the house while Welks followed them in a bemused way.

When they were settled in the carriage, Lord Tregarthan gathered Jane into his arms. 'Now, my love, your mother forbids the marriage. No! Don't speak yet. Your father does not, but I cannot wait to get his written permission. I have bought you some clothes and I shall buy you more as we journey north. Mrs Hart will not pursue us. She will remain behind to make the best of it. Now, what have you to say?'

'Nothing!' laughed Jane. 'Except, yes, my lord.'

'Rupert. My name is Rupert.'

'Yes, Rupert.'

'Then remove that silly bonnet so that I can kiss you properly. Oh, Jane. *Beautiful* Jane!'

Welks, as Lord Tregarthan had known he was bound to do, confided in the first footman. The first footman told Abraham, and Abraham found an excuse to escape to Clarges Street at the first possible opportunity. The staff with the exception of Joseph were too sad over Rainbird's departure to care very much, but Joseph went to The Running Footman with the gossip and soon London society knew that Jane Hart had eloped with Lord Tregarthan and had the enjoyable task of telling Mrs Hart all about it.

Mrs Hart had strong hysterics and took to her bed. Lord Tregarthan was well aware that she would be in social disgrace when it was found that her daughter had deemed it necessary to elope with one of London's most marriageable men. He had felt she deserved to suffer for her treatment of Jane.

Euphemia pretended she did not care, but she began to care very much when Mrs Hart finally roused from her sickbed to declare her intention of leaving town, then rounded on Euphemia and blamed the girl for being a waste of time and money. If Euphemia wanted to find a husband, she would need to be content with hunting one down at the Brighton assemblies. There was nothing to stop their return to Upper Patchett. Mrs Blewett had already left, claiming that the house was too damp, and saying that Lady Doyle, after extracting a large sum of money, which she said she was going to present to the church so that they might build a hall named after Mrs Blewett, had disappeared altogether and was rumoured to be in Ireland.

In vain did Euphemia weep and beg. Mrs Hart had had enough. People were beginning to cut her again, and she was sure Jane would return ruined and unmarried. Number 67 Clarges Street was unlucky, she said to all who would listen. Only look what had happened to her? Her husband gone to sea, her daughter run off, a murderer found dead in the hall, and Euphemia, for all her great beauty, still unwed.

Rainbird walked along Lanceton Street in Brighton. There were small villas on either side with pocket-sized gardens. He stopped outside Number 11 and studied the house. It belonged, Lord Tregarthan had told him, to a Mrs Peters, a widow who was a friend of Felice and who had known her parents.

He straightened his cravat with nervous fingers, picked up his portmanteau, and opened the gate.

A seagull wheeled and screamed overhead and he could smell the sea.

He knocked at the door and waited.

Felice's second name was Laurent. He had practised saying it many times with a French accent, but when a stout middle-aged woman opened the door, he stammered out that he would like to see 'Miss Lawrahnt.'

The woman smiled, asked his name, and then left, shutting the door in his face.

He waited impatiently. What a long time she seemed to be taking!

At last she opened the door again and invited him inside to a tiny, dark hall. She held open a door.

Rainbird walked into a small, cluttered parlour.

Felice was sitting in front of the fire. She looked exactly as she had before, wearing the same brown silk dress she had worn in Clarges Street and with the same smooth wings of hair framing her face. Rainbird stood helplessly, choked by a wave of emotion.

'Sit down, John,' said Felice placidly. 'It is good to see you. I am sorry I ran away without saying goodbye but I felt sure I would be amply rewarded for my services – and I was.'

'So you have a dowry,' said Rainbird heavily, for it struck him that Felice might think he only wanted to marry her to get his hands on it.

'Yes, I have a dowry,' she said, bending her head over her stitching. 'I hope to make an advantageous marriage.'

Rainbird winced. 'You must have had many

adventures,' he said, 'with Captain Hart and Lord Tregarthan.'

'Yes, it was all most uncomfortable. The good captain was kind, but that man Tregarthan! Bah. He had no thought for my safety or comfort. He ordered me about like a trooper.'

'He is to marry Miss Jane,' said Rainbird. 'They are going to elope, I think. He asked me to leave miss with him, and his travelling carriage was outside. Oh, we have had such dramas.' He told her about Mr Gillespie and the murder of Clara.

'*Tiens!*' said Felice, much amused. 'That Tregarthan! His beloved is nearly murdered on the one day and he drags her off on an elopement the next. He is lucky Miss Jane is not missish.'

'I gather his lordship has been very generous to you,' said Rainbird, wishing she would put down her sewing and look at him.

'I earned it,' said Felice dryly. 'What brings you here, John?'

'You,' said Rainbird.

Felice's busy hands stilled and she smoothed the piece of sewing on her lap. She looked up, her gaze calm and steady. 'It would not answer, John,' she said. 'You and I. Marriage is not for us. I am tired of servitude and insecurity. I shall marry a comfortable middle-aged burgher and bear him children. Love is a luxury I cannot afford.'

'Please, Felice,' said Rainbird, sinking to one knee in front of her.

'No, my butler friend. No. You English are so

romantic. In France we are used to marriages of convenience at every level of society. Besides, you have too many responsibilities. All those children!'

'I do not have children, Felice. I have never been married.'

'I mean MacGregor, Joseph, Dave, Mrs Middleton, Alice, Jenny, and Lizzie – *those* children. You will never really desert them.'

'For you – only for you – would I desert them.'

'*Menteur!*' laughed Felice. 'How you lie, and yet you think you are telling the truth.' She put her sewing aside. 'But you may say goodbye to me properly.' She took his hands and rose, drawing him up to his feet. 'Come,' she said softly.

Bemused, Rainbird followed her out of the parlour and up a dark wooden staircase to her bedroom above. 'You can't mean,' he said, 'you can't . . .'

'I can,' smiled Felice, unfastening the tapes of her gown. 'This is a farewell present, John. Come and take it . . . now.'

The next evening Rainbird alighted from the Brighton coach at Blossom's Inn, Lawrence Lane in the City. The sun had set and a purplish smoky sky stretched above the roof-tops.

Rainbird bought a bottle of brandy with some of his savings, all of which he had taken with him in the hope of starting a new life with Felice. He decided to walk. His heart felt heavy and the very thought of returning to Clarges Street made him miserable. A smell of sassafras, sugar, and hot milk rose from the saloop stalls at the corners of the winding City streets.

Number 67 *was* unlucky, decided Rainbird bitterly. Murder had been done there, suicide, financial ruin – and even Fiona Sinclair, she who had married the Earl of Harrington and had seemed all set to have a happy life, had disappeared.

Rainbird decided to call at Hanover Square on the road home and ask if there was any news of the Earl and Countess of Harrington. The familiar, unpleasant, fat white face of the Harringtons' butler peered round the door. 'What d'ye want?' demanded Lord Harrington's butler nastily.

'Is there any news of the earl and countess?' asked Rainbird.

'They was found in Turkey by Mr Sinclair,' said the butler.

'Well?' asked Rainbird breathlessly.

''Er ladyship was sick o' something furren and they was staying with this pasha and the letters never got 'ome. But we 'as one now, and they're all right, so push off.'

Rainbird walked lightly with his springy acrobat's step across Hanover Square. Surely the bad luck of the house was over. Fiona was safe. Perhaps, just perhaps, if he returned to Brighton, say, in a month's time, Felice might have changed her mind. He could write to her. At least he could do that!

As he approached Number 67, he heard the twanging of Joseph's mandolin soaring up in the night air.

Rainbird ran quickly down the area steps. 'I'm back,' he called cheerfully. 'Everybody . . . I'm home.'

Lord Tregarthan removed his bride's white satin wedding gown, held it out at arm's length, and looked at it with a critical eye. 'Definitely got the stamp of the village dress-maker,' he said. 'Well, my sweet, we shall be married again in church in London when we eventually return and then you may have a proper wedding gown.'

Jane stood in her shift, shivering with a mixture of apprehension, desire, and nerves. 'Do you mean to stand there all night examining my wardrobe?' she asked sharply.

He tossed the gown into the corner and took her in his arms. 'No, my love,' he said, his eyes glinting with laughter. 'I have other plans . . . like this . . . and this . . . and this . . .

A stormy hour ensued. Jane, lying at last with her head against his naked chest, murmured, 'Poor mama. How very upset she must be.'

'She will forgive us . . . unfortunately. At this moment, I confess I find that the idea of never having to see your mama again would please me very much.'

'I would like to see papa,' said Jane. 'I know *he* will be happy for me.'

'As soon as we hear of his return, we will travel to meet his ship. In the meantime, we have all the time in the world to ourselves.'

'I feel so safe,' yawned Jane. 'I must have been mad to try to catch Mr Gillespie by myself. I . . . I thought you would be so proud of me, but you have never stopped complaining about it.'

'And never shall,' he said lazily. 'When I think of the peril you were in with only those odd servants to help you.'

'They are most unusual,' said Jane. 'And so very brave and loyal. When I first met them, I thought they must be related in some way. Rainbird, the butler, asked me to give the staff references should I ever find myself a lady of consequence.'

'And so you are, and so you shall. But you will never need to ask them for help again. I shall make very sure if anyone dies a mysterious death that you are not allowed to become curious.

'So forget the horrors of poor Clara's death, and kiss me again . . . *beautiful* Jane.'